Embers of Evil

FIREMEN in asbestos garments crouched behind shields in an attempt to brave that awful heat and reach the flames with water that changed to steam almost before it struck!

As they raced nearer, a fire truck swung wildly away from the fire zone and raced toward them and, even as it fled, flames burst out beneath it, swept over it and, in one vast enveloping explosion, engulfed the entire piece of equipment. A man's high, tearing scream wailed to them out of the night. And the truck was running wild down the street!

With a wrench that almost capsized the limousine, Kirkpatrick's driver skidded into a sidestreet, as the blazing truck raced past. Wentworth saw the flaming Juggernaut leap high as it sprang across the curb and heard the crash as it slammed into a store window. An instant later, a shattering explosion drove in the windows of the limousine, popped them into glittering shards. For half a block, Kirkpatrick's car reeled crazily as the chauffeur fought the effects of the concussion. His brakes howled, and he jerked the lumbering car to a halt within inches of a lamp post, slumped forward over the wheel.

Kirkpatrick sprang to the street, but Wentworth hauled him back and climbed behind the wheel of the car.

"That was an accident," he called, and his voice sounded dull and flat in his own ears.

Kirkpatrick swore at him raggedly, "Accident? Accident?"

Wentworth had the car rolling, throwing words back over his shoulder. "We can't help here! Up there, near the fire somewhere, are the men who started it! They had a reason. Robbery. When we find the reason, we'll find the men."

THE SPIDER

MASTER OF MEN!

™

ABOVE THE LAW ... SWORN ENEMY OF THE UNDERWORLD ... HATED BY BOTH ...

The Full-Length SPIDER Novel

MASTER of the FLAMING HORDE

By NORVELL PAGE
(writing as Grant Stockbridge)

A mass-murder weapon, too horrible for war, was sweeping New York with fire—under the barbaric, pitiless direction of the Master of the Flame Men! First warning of the unseen cloud of death was a breath of tainted air that transformed a sombre populace into a laughing, drunken riot. Then came a blast that would smash a skyscraper into bits... From the charred and twisted embers of the towering holocaust, Richard Wentworth rose, in the fear-inspiring guise of the *Spider*, to smoke the arson assassin out from behind the machine guns of his flame-cloaked bodyguard—and fight for the lives of a reeling, giggling people too blind-drunk to flee!

~ EDITED BY RICH HARVEY ~

COVER PAINTING BY JOHN HOWITT • STORY ILLUSTRATIONS BY J. FLEMING GOULD

BOLD VENTURE PRESS • BORDENTOWN, NJ

THE SPIDER #50:

MASTER OF THE FLAMING HORDE

~ a BOLD VENTURE PRESS book ~

published by arrangement with
Argosy Communications, Inc.

Originally published in THE SPIDER Magazine, November 1937
Bold Venture Press edition / November 2001

Edited and Produced by
RICH HARVEY

Front Cover Production
NEIL MECHEM

Created by
HARRY STEEGER

ISBN: 0-9712246-1-7

Bold Venture Press
Post Office Box 64 • Bordentown, NJ 08505
boldventurepress@aol.com
Printed in the USA

~ *Conducted for the Spider* ~
By CHRISTOPHER R. YATES

"Not Your Father's Pulp Hero"

FOR those who just cracked the spine of a Spider paperback in the last five to ten years — what seasoned hero pulp fans would call a "newbie" — The Spider is not your father's adventure hero. He's your grandfather's!

Born in the depression era and out of print before D-Day, the people who bought *Spider* magazines straight from the newsstands are easily in their 70s or 80s now.

The "newbie's" parents, adults in the decades of the 1960s and 1970s, saw a total of eight *Spider* magazine reprints — and half of those were badly edited and miserably "updated" for the 1970s readership. Consequently, parents today likely never knew of the Master of Men when his stories were readily available.

However, from the mid-1980s to present day roughly forty of the original 118 published *Spider* adventures have been reprinted — many of these include encores of the original pulp magazine illustrations. The print runs are smaller, and the distribution could be broader, but the *Spider* is back. What was old is now new. As it turns out, your grandpa was a pretty cool guy.

My grandfather introduced me to "the pulps." Every time I mentioned my beloved comic book heroes he would predictably sing the praises of the "real heroes" exploding from titles like Argosy and All-Story and including guys by the names of Tarzan, Zorro, and, of course, The Shadow. At that tender young age, still under the spell of caped crusaders with their garish costumes and word bubbles, I truly thought my grandpa had a profoundly dull taste in fiction.

Then I grew up, went to college, then law school and spent the better part of a decade as a city attorney defending firefighters and police officers from lawsuits. A particular breed of lawsuit — although not common — really gets under my skin. Sometimes the criminal gets busted just seconds before they actually complete their crime. For example, the cops arrive just before the senile old lady/robbery victim can hand her cash to the thug. The officers make the arrest and begin to prosecute the villain. But wait, the senile old lady never had the chance to lose her dough.

By the strict legal definition, she really wasn't robbed. Charges are dropped and then the robber sues the arresting officers for everything they own on the basis of false arrest and malicious prosecution. The worst part of it is that sometimes the criminals succeed.

IN LIGHT of courtroom experiences like these, comic books just could not offer the sort of escapism I needed. The Man of Steel is way too busy saving the universe from alien invasion to even care that a well meaning police officer has to sell his home to pay a court judgment to a petty thief. For the first time, my grandpa's "real heroes" started to look appealing. By comparison, superheroes now seem ridiculous.

The contrived angst, the fairy tale plots, the bright capes and long underwear, it all got old. Of all the pulp heroes to pick from, The Spider just met my fictional needs much better. The Master of Men stands apart from, and above, his caped descendents on the basis of two fundamentals of hero fiction — he actually stops the bad guy —permanently — and his dual identity just makes sense.

To elaborate, the *Spider* does what no comic book hero would dare do. He sticks to the bad guys like a cheap suit and executes them. Dead guys don't sue. You can quibble about the need or usefulness of capital punishment, but the bottom line is that the folks the *Spider* put down made Hannibal Lecter look like a

girl scout. Admit it, they deserved every bullet. Now compare The Spider's villains to the Joker, for example. That giggling whack-job has spent over sixty years pointlessly slaughtering any man, woman or child unfortunate enough to cross his path. Is he pushing up daises? No way.

Or how about your friendly neighborhood Spider-Man? Think about what he does to criminals. Your average New York City police officer comes upon some unfortunate loser swinging upside down from a light post all cozy in an oversized spider web. No evidence, no witnesses, no victim. And a confession? If you were facing five to ten in the pokey would you let some smart mouth teenager in long johns intimidate you into fessing up? Didn't think so. I could go on, but let's just say the Orkin man does a far better job eliminating vermin than our super buddies in brightly colored underwear.

The *Spider* doesn't just pick the bad guys off; he does a pretty good job of scaring the hell out of them first. He does this with a very effective use of his dual identity — yet another element of hero fiction where comic book super heroes fail to make the grade.

FOR EXAMPLE, let's ponder the Dark Knight. Really now, does Batman's costume strike terror in the hearts of evildoers? Of course not. You see a guy in armor plated undies with a ribbed cape and a cowl, you're not scared — you want to snap a picture and sell it to the *National Enquirer*. Don't even get me started on Robin's outfit.

Now how would you feel if you ran into a guy dressed in black with a hunchback, wild, scraggily hair, fangs and two 45-caliber pistols pointed at you? Be honest now; evildoer or goodie-two-shoes, it doesn't matter, you would lose continence and run like a sissy.

And then there is the matter of a "secret identity." Richard Wentworth is the *Spider*. His true love, Nita Van Sloan knows it. As does Wentworth's butler (Jenkyns), chauffer (Jackson) and side-kick (Ram Singh). The police commissioner, Stanley Kirkpatrick, knows it too. He just can't prove it. Most of the *Spider's* worthy enemies eventually figure out who's behind the fangs and fedora also. When you ponder this point, it just makes sense. Greasepaint and face putty can only fool you for so long.

So what's Superman's secret? How is it that hapless Lois can work with Clark nine hours a day, five to seven days a week and not be able to make the connection between her co-worker and the Man of Steel? Come on now, Superman's corn fed, midwestern face is out there for the entire world to see. Could a pair of non-prescription glasses really hide anything? You know the answer.

L ET'S FACE it; the *Spider* is hands down way cooler than any comic book hero. Your grandfather wasn't sucked in by the lure of the four-color panel and spandex. When he was young the bad guys routinely died of lead poisoning and folks who ran around in their underwear were locked up and given lobotomies. The *Spider* was your grandfather's kind of hero. He is, or should be, the hero of players in the legal system like me who yearn for a different type of justice.

With this fantastic reprint in your hand, you might just agree with me.

— *Christopher R. Yates*

Art: Raphael DeSoto

Master of the

by
NORVELL PAGE

(Writing as "Grant Stockbridge")

Over Manhattan's dizzy towers fell that insidious invisible menace—an unseen cloud of death that first transformed the entire metropolis into a laughing, drunken riot and then blasted it to bits! Who was the evil Master of these Flame Men, who had found a red way to amass millions by gutting New York with fire? In defense of those reeling, giggling victims, trapped in their awesome death-spree, Richard Wentworth, in the Spider's weird robes, rose from the charred embers—to fight his greatest battle against an arson assassin no one had ever seen—for a doomed people so blind-drunk they could not see!

Flaming Horde

A Feature-Length *Spider* Novel

CHAPTER ONE
On Death's Trail

WENTWORTH bent sharply forward as the heavy Daimler pushed through the chill gust from the river. His eyes, keen with suspicion, stabbed at an unlighted car that was stationary on the dark sidestreet. Afterward, he settled back, but did not relax. His frown changed to a smile, as he turned to the woman beside him.

He said casually, "I'm jumpy as a cat."

Nita van Sloan also had a small from between her satiny black brows. "Whom do you think you're fooling?" she asked impatiently. "You didn't maneuver this invitation to the Spanish Consulate for the pleasure of Don Carlos' company. Or have you decided to carry your sword-

In one vast enveloping blast, firemen and trucks were engulfed in flames.

cane even on social occasions now?"

Wentworth's smile became slightly grim. "I'm glad my enemies are not so astute as you, dear," he acknowledged. "Martinez phoned that Don Carlos seemed ... *frightened* when he learned we were coming."

"Frightened?"

Wentworth nodded. "There have been certain rumors from Spanish sympathizers about a new weapon of war which even the Spanish hesitated to use, and..." He broke off sharply, as his chauffeur called softly to him.

"Sahib!" the man said. "A car follows us!"

"Thank you, Ram Singh," Wentworth acknowledged, "I know." His eyes lingered for a moment on the man's broad shoulders and alertly erect turbaned head, and a suspicion of a smile touched his chiseled lips again. "My Sikh scents battle," he murmured to Nita. The smile faded. "I had hoped I was wrong. If criminals here get hold of that weapon, and—"

Nita's hand closed sharply on his arm. "Look, Dick!" she cried. "Isn't that Martinez?"

Wentworth stared where she pointed. Ram Singh was already curving to the curb before the consul's home and the man Nita indicated was not fifty feet from the entrance. But he was walking in the opposite direction, if his progress could be called walking. He was staggering, reeling like a drunken man. And he was laughing loudly. Even through the closed windows and above the mutter of the powerful engine, Wentworth could hear his laughter. It didn't seem possible that this could be the grave and dignified Martinez! The man braced a hand against a lamp post and threw back his head in exultant laughter and for a moment his profile stood out, strong and hawkish.

"By the heavens!" Wentworth cried. "It *is* Martinez!"

His hand snapped to the door-catch, but he hesitated. There was something strange about this. Martinez was behaving like a drunken man, like a crazy man, and yet he had been grave, even apprehensive, when he had phoned a short while before. Wentworth's eyes flashed to the rear-vision mirror, saw the pursuing car jerk to a halt, a half block behind. Three men spewed from it!

Wentworth was instantly in action. With a shout of warning to Nita van Sloan, he snatched an automatic from a compartment in the car and sprang to the pavement.

"Ram Singh!" he called sharply. "Get the *missie sahib* inside! On thy head be it!"

HE SCARCELY waited for the rumbling answer, but went striding toward Martinez, gun ready in his hand. The three men skulked in the darkness like waiting wolves. It was as if they guessed with what deadly accuracy that gun could blast, as if they knew that they had more to deal with than the ordinary wealthy man-about-town Wentworth appeared to be.

Yet they could not know that he was secretly... the *Spider!* Had they guessed that, they would have fled in terror rather than followed his trail! For the *Spider* administered his own dread justice. Let any criminal sin against humanity and, as surely as death itself, he would find that cloaked and fateful nemesis, the *Spider,* upon his trail! For him, there could be but one end to that trail—swift and ruthless execution!

Grimly, Wentworth strode to Martinez' side while his gun bore steadily on those three bunched men.

"What's the matter, my friend?" Wentworth asked quietly. "Are you ill?"

"Que diablo!" Martinez gasped. "Ill? I never felt better! But it seems to me three dogs skulk there in the shadows! Let us flog them, *amigo!"*

Wentworth stared narrowly into Martinez' face and, with a curious sense of dread, he felt something of the man's exhilaration creep into his own blood. His breathing was more rapid and he sensed a peculiar and stimulating freshness in the air. He caught Martinez' arm.

"Come away!" he ordered sharply. "There's treachery here!"

Martinez wrenched free and staggered on uncertain feet, and Wentworth felt, with a rising apprehension, an almost overwhelming impulse to laugh, felt a swaggering strength that prompted him, too, to battle! Coldness crept up his back. There was something fiendish here!

"Martinez!" His voice rasped. "Come inside. At once! This is a trap of some sort. It—"

A shot from the shadows where the men lurked cut him short. Wentworth heard the bullet whisper by, and his reaction was lightning swift. With a straight-arm thrust, he sent Martinez reeling out of the spot of light beneath the street lamp, leaped clear and flung himself to earth as he snapped out an answering shot ....

It was precisely as if the flash of his gun exploded the whole night into flame!

A searing gust struck Wentworth across the face, spun him rolling along the street for a dozen feet. He heard a woman's scream and then a man was shrieking terribly. For a moment, he had the crazy idea that his automatic had exploded suddenly in his own hand. He tried to thrust himself to his feet and failed, brought his mighty will into play and reeled erect, stood swaying groggily. His faltering, half-blinded eyes swept over the street, and for the first time since the blast, he saw Martinez. It was Martinez who was shrieking—no, screaming like a woman—in nameless terror!

Martinez was running with great bounding strides, and nothing of him could be seen at all. He was wrapped from head to foot in a cloak of flames that seemed to feed upon his very flesh! As Wentworth fought his numbed senses, and took the first faltering steps forward to help, he saw Martinez slam against a brick wall and rebound, still screaming, whirl and race blindly in the opposite direction across the street. Wentworth tried to shout, to call him, and sound scarcely passed his lips. Martinez fell, and after a moment the screams stopped, though the flames still danced brightly above him— though they twirled and flapped and flaunted their torturing spires gaily above him.

Wentworth tugged at his coat, ran on wooden, stumbling feet toward where Martinez lay. It was hopeless to attempt to blot out those flames. He knew, too, that Martinez must already be dead and beyond the torture of the fire, and yet he must try. He was almost beside the body before he remembered that three assassins lurked near-by and that one of them had fired on him!

With the thought, he wheeled fumblingly about. The three men were closing in on him. With a sense of unreality, Wentworth saw that, instead of guns, each man gripped a long-bladed knife. And, strangely, Wentworth laughed!

DANGER cleared his head like a clean wind. In an instant, the cobwebs of shock were swept away and his keen eyes stabbed about him. His gun had fallen from his hand at the time of the blast, but if he could hold these killers at bay for a few moments, Ram Singh would join the battle, and then.... Wentworth's eyes widened, and he bit back a savage curse. There would be no help from Ram Singh! The doughty Sikh had returned too soon to the fight.

He lay limply against the wall across the street, plainly hurled there by the explosion. There were two people, a couple, near the consulate itself, but they were wrapped in each other's arms in terror and could do nothing except summon the police—and that would come too late!

Even as he realized his augmented peril, the three knifemen closed in with a rush!

On the instant, Wentworth sprang into action. With a prodigious backward leap, he cleared the still burning body of Martinez and snatched up his smoldering coat. He flung the flaming garment squarely into the face of the nearest man and, in its wake, leaped to the attack! Even with the speed of his movements, Wentworth had not acted without deliberation. He concentrated on the man at the extreme left of the three assailants, so that, for the time it would take the others to circle. he would have no enemies at his back.

Almost in the same instant that the coat struck the end man, Wentworth was upon him! A wrench gave him the assassin's knife, but he did not at once relinquish his wrist hold. Wentworth stepped aside and forward and, using the momentum of his own attack, whirled the knifeman over his shoulder in a flying mare. The man screamed out once hoarsely, then he crashed into a second man and bore him to the earth. Once more Wentworth laughed and there was triumph in his voice. It was characteristic of him that he gambled his entire safety on one swift move. With a quick flip of his wrist, he hurled the knife he had seized straight at the last of his enemies!

The throw was beautifully timed, perfectly executed, but the knifeman was an instant too quick. His own blade was whistling through the air before Wentworth's left his hand. Wentworth dodged. The knife snagged through the shoulder of his shirt, but his own throw went wild. And before he could spring into action again, a kick from one of those he had spilled knocked his feet from under him.

As Wentworth plunged toward the pavement, he knew a sharp sense of disaster. It was not alone that he was fighting, unarmed, against three killers with small hope of winning. It was the realization of the amount of time that had elapsed since the blast without police reaching the scene. Except for the consulate, the neighborhood was virtually deserted at this hour of the evening, but surely someone within the building would have phoned an alarm unless . . . unless they were in the conspiracy! Good God, and Nita was inside there, had gone at his orders ....

It was a flash of thought in the midst of peril, but it did not slow his fighting. He was rolling even before he hit the ground, rolling toward his assailants! He had small hope of being able to dodge a second throw in this vague light and his only chance was to close as quickly as possible with his enemies. In that way, he might hope to wrest another knife from one of them or to use his swift fists to advantage.

He had a glimpse of two men on their feet, a third struggling to rise. Out of the corner of his eye, he saw a kick aimed at his head—too late to dodge. The blow crashed against his temple. Dazed and blinded, Wentworth still fought on. His fingers closed around an ankle and yanked. He struck out with his feet. Momentarily, he expected the stinging punch of a stabbing knife against his ribs. He ....

Good Lord! Someone was shooting! He could hear the heavy blasts of a gun, but could feel no blow of bullets.

DIZZILY, Wentworth struggled up, peered about him. Two men were running toward their auto. They carried the third between them. Across the street, a man was prone on the sidewalk beside a woman. Even as Wentworth stared, a gun in the man's hand spurted flame toward the three assassins.

On rubbery legs, Wentworth lumbered toward those two on the sidewalk. Plainly, this was the couple he had noticed earlier near the consulate. But for their help ....

"Don't shoot!" Wentworth called hoarsely. "Let them go!"

He was within a half dozen yards of the man now. The assassins were scrambling into their car. Wentworth tried to drive his body to greater speed. He was fumbling in his pocket, and the white faces of the two on the sidewalk turned up toward him.

"You saved my life," Wentworth panted. "No time even to thank you. My card, here. Please get that Hindu to the hospital. Come to my home as soon as you can. Stay lying down where you are. Those killers ..."

Wentworth looped about and was sprinting for his Daimler. His brain was clearer despite the damnable thumping in his skull. He knew what he had to do. Behind him, a motor bellowed into life. A gun blasted and lead slammed into the door of the Daimler, as Wentworth

wrenched it open and dived in behind the wheel. There was no key in the ignition lock, but he had one in his pockets. Precious moments were lost while he fumbled, eyes straining in the rear-vision mirror. The killers' car was rolling, roaring toward him, but the Daimler was bullet-proof. The *key!*

Wentworth jabbed at the lock, and a storm of bullets drummed against the door and window beside him. He jerked and slammed sideways to the seat . . . Moments later, when the assassin car squealed around a corner, Wentworth kicked the starter and set the powerful Daimler rolling. The killers thought they had left him dead. They wouldn't expect immediate pursuit. Wentworth's lips set in a grim line.

His brain was already racing with a thousand conjectures. His narrow escape from death, which might have left a lesser man dazed and intimidated, was already thrust aside—as was the fact of Nita van Sloan's apparent captivity in the consulate. Nothing less would have kept her from dashing to his aid. However, with the knowledge that Wentworth still lived, they would not dare to hurt the woman he loved. He hoped they wouldn't! Ram Singh...But Ram Singh might be dead! Yet these personal matters must wait. The *Spider* was on the trail!

At memory of Martinez' hideous death, Wentworth's face grew bleak. Of the way in which that doom had been accomplished he had no idea, but one thing he did know. If Martinez had been killed, as he suspected, by means of the awful Spanish weapon of war of which he had heard, his worst fears were confirmed. It had been brought to America. It was in criminal hands, and those criminals were ruthless. God pity the people of America, if the chase of the *Spider* tonight met failure!

WENTWORTH'S eyes lanced ahead to the fugitive car. The frantic speed of its first flight was diminished. The Daimler slowed, too. Wentworth had no wish to overtake the men, nor to wreak a petty vengeance. He had shouted to the man who had saved him to let them go— so that the Spider could follow them to their masters!

Abruptly, Wentworth spun the Daimler into a sidestreet and the motor moaned with mounting speed. He must not alarm his prey by too close or obvious pursuit. For a space of blocks he ran a parallel course, watching for the quarry at the cross-streets. When once more, he took the direct trail, he was burning a different set of lights. For at night, a car was chiefly identifiable by its lights.

The course of the chase wound eastward to the river, then to the south. Wentworth was once more following a parallel route when the quarry failed to reappear at an intersection. Swiftly, he spun the Daimler into the cross-street. Before he reached the corner, the other car droned past in second gear and by the brief gleam of the street lights, Wentworth saw that only one man remained in it. Although he flashed across the corner only a moment later, Wentworth was too late to spot the building into which the other two men had vanished. He would have to work fast!

The sidestreet in which Wentworth parked was pitch-dark, nor did any light escape from the tonneau when he had drawn the curtains. Pressure on a hidden button caused half the rear seat to slide slowly forward, revealing a compact wardrobe and a mirrored tray which became a brilliantly lighted make-up table in an instant.

Minutes were precious. He doubted that the pair would leave their hideout soon—since one was wounded they would go only to a haven, or the headquarters from which they worked—but Wentworth could not depend on that. He would strike swiftly, but it must be as the *Spider* that he delivered the blow!

Deftly, he applied a liquid to his entire face. It sallowed the skin and drew it tautly over the bones and the bridge of his nose. Shadow deepened the lines and hollows of his face and putty turned the nose into a hawk-like and predatory beak. His mouth became a lipless gash. Shaggy eyebrows, a lank black wig—and the face of the *Spider* glared back at Wentworth from the mirror. A black shirt and dark tweed coat, a black cape about his shoulders, and Wentworth snatched a black slouch hat from the wardrobe. He jabbed his hand into the card compartment for the second gun he always kept there—but it came out *empty!*

Impatiently, Wentworth snapped on a thread of light from a pocket flash. Grimness settled about his mouth. Ram Singh must have taken the second weapon! Well, so be it. Wentworth did not hesitate. He could not. Too much depended on swift action. He snatched up the sword-cane which still was in the car, punched open the door and stepped out into the shadows, became one with them. Unarmed, perhaps into the very headquarters of the killers itself, the *Spider* went forth to battle!

CHAPTER TWO
What Lies Waiting?

THE ROOM was dingy and cold, and the dim electric bulb threw more shadows than light across the bed where a man lay moaning. He was small, but thickly built. His face was swarthy. Another man bent over him.

"Be quiet, Manuel!" he cried in hissing Spanish to the injured one. "The police can hear you two blocks away."

Manuel swore at him. "My leg is broken, Juan," he groaned. "But it is not simply that. The master say to knife this *Señor* Wentworth and then to burn him. And the fool required shooting. The master will not like that. And *por dios!* When he does not like a thing it is bad— very bad for someone! Do you forget how that poor Alfredo screamed in the fire?"

The man called Juan shrugged, but his swarthy face was pale. "I do not forget," he muttered. *"Por dios,* no!" He sat down on the side of the bed and began to build a cigarette. His fingers were strangely awkward about the task and his eyes strained in the effort to focus. He spilled some tobacco and watched it fall. He giggled. Once he had started he did not seem able to stop. He giggled until the wounded Manuel cackled, too.

"I do not worry!" Juan said thickly. "I feel very fine. It is as if I had drunk much good wine!"

Manuel swore through his laughter. His face was suffused, his eyes oddly bright. "Me, I do not worry either! Tomorrow we have *mucho dinero* for this little killing tonight. You will find me a girl, eh?" His breath came very quickly. *"Por dios!* I am a man! With a broken leg, I can think of a woman!"

The men laughed uproariously. Juan got to his feet and staggered about the room, singing off-key in a high nasal voice. Manuel was not watching him. He stared before him with queerly bright eyes.

"Do you notice, *amigo,"* he said thickly, "how good the air smells? It is like the air after a thunder shower when there has been much lightning." He breathed in deeply, began to laugh again, the sound thin and foolish like a young girl's. "Did you observe, *amigo,"* he asked, "how this Martinez laughed and laughed before he died?"

Manuel threw back his head and laughed, and did not notice that his own mirth was strangely like the crazy laughter of Martinez. It was while he still was laughing that the door whipped open and a man sprang inside, a black cape swirling from his shoulders, eyes burning coldly beneath the wide brim of his black hat. It was the *Spider!*

BEFORE the door had jarred against the wall, the Spider had Juan by the throat and had borne him to his knees. He shook the man violently, hurled him across the room before he heeled the door shut and picked up his cane from the floor. Then he faced the two killers, a hunched, malevolent figure with the bared steel of a sword-cane in his fist!

"Dogs!" whispered the *Spider,* his Spanish rolling like a death-drum. "Dogs who think yourselves wolves! Which of you chooses to die first!"

Juan crouched on the floor where he had been hurled, a snarl showing his discolored teeth. His hand slid stealthily beneath his shirt. Manuel trembled so that the bed creaked.

"Santa Maria!" he whispered. "It is the devil himself!"

The *Spider* laughed—a flat mocking sound. "Come for your souls, assassins! Where is your master?"

Wentworth's eyes bore harshly on those of his prisoners, but he was also watching Juan's sly reach for his knife. His ears were strained to catch the first whisper of movement in the hallways of the slattern tenement. It had been simple to follow a blood-drop trail to this room, but hurried search had revealed no trace of a murder headquarters. Still, there might be hidden allies near; the man who had gone on with the car might return... As yet, Wentworth had not sensed the peculiar freshness of the air in the room and the two killers no longer laughed as Martinez had laughed ....

"Fools, speak!" the *Spider* ordered raspingly. "Where is your master?"

Juan came tensely to his feet, laughed in sudden bravado—and once more there was a curiously drunken note.

"If you are the devil," he said thickly, "you should know! I do not believe you are the devil! No. You are ..." His hand flicked from his shirt with the knife, whipped back to throw. Quick as he was, the *Spider's* sword was swifter. Body and arm straightened in a lunge that carried him half across the room. Juan gave a hoarse scream. His hand stiffened against the wall, pinned there by the sword point. The knife rang on the floor.

As swiftly as he had struck, Wentworth recovered. With his dripping sword point, he sketched a swift design upon the floor, a figure of eight hairy legs around a malignant body, of poised, venomous fangs—*the seal of the Spider!* Juan gasped a curse and Manuel cringed upon the bed.

"You!" gasped Manuel. *"You! Por dios,* I would rather face the devil!"

Juan moaned and sank to his knees, a prayer pattering from his lips.

"Where is your master?" Wentworth repeated softly. He felt, as once before tonight, a strange sense of exhilaration, a curious urge to laughter. "Speak, fools! The *Spider* commands you!"

Manuel giggled. He tried to strangle the sound, and burst out into crazy laughter. Juan stared at him a moment, then cackled, too.

"You command us!" Manuel choked. "You command us? Do you know who I am—I, Manuel? You..." He broke off with a hissing curse and, suddenly, a revolver was in his hand, snatched from somewhere about his person, and leveled at Wentworth's stomach.

Wentworth choked back a curse. Was his eyesight failing that be had not seen the man's quick movement? His brain felt extraordinarily clear, and yet ....

The curse forced itself out. He had felt this way tonight ... when Martinez had died!

"Don't shoot, you fool," he cried, "or you will die as Martinez died! Can't you smell it in the air?"

"It is trickery!" Juan snarled. "Slay him, Manuel!"

Behind him, Wentworth grasped the knob of the door, yet dared not attempt to escape. It was not the bullet he feared. He remembered how his own shot, a short while before, had filled the night with flame, had wrapped Martinez in a fiery cloak of death! If a gun were fired here ....

"Wait!" he cried. "Have you done anything to displease your master? Think hard! He is planning to destroy you as he did Martinez!"

The *Spider* had small hope of keeping Manuel from shooting. The man was drunk—drunk on whatever was this thing in the air that could turn a man's flesh into fuel. His own brain seemed afire but dull ... dull. Behind him, he slowly turned the door knob, and the effort seemed to require enormous concentration. It was almost impossible to keep talking while he worked.

"Listen to me," he went on feverishly. "When I came in you were laughing— as Martinez laughed before he died. Do you remember? If you fire that gun, you will both die! Don't you understand? Manuel, put down that gun!"

For a moment, the man hesitated. His face was twisted with the effort at thought, and the strange laughter worked in his throat and made his breath come noisily. Wentworth had turned the latch of the door now. A quick movement might throw him outside the room. But if he could make Manuel even lower that gun....

"Throw down that gun," he insisted, "before you kill us all!"

Juan cursed as Manuel burst into sudden laughter. "It is a trick, fool!" Juan cried. "Shoot! Shoot, now!"

Wentworth caught the flickering change in Manuel's face and knew that he would fire. On the instant, Wentworth flung himself into swift action. He jerked open the door, flung himself bodily backward through the opening. As he fell, he whipped the cape forward and up over his face. It was while he was still falling that the gun spoke!

THE blast seemed to pick Wentworth up and hurl him through space. His breath was driven back into his lungs, and intolerable heat swept over him. He knew vaguely that he was hurtling through the air, and he curled his head forward, tried to make himself into a ball. A blow across his shoulders drove the breath from him. Wentworth lay still.

His brain was still hazily aware of sound about him ... screams and hoarse shouts. He tried to thrust himself up and seemed unable to move a finger.

Wentworth knew presently that he was flat on his back on the floor, that the shouts of people were diminishing, dying out in the deeper roar of the flames. The air about him was thick with black smoke that swirled and roiled above his head.

Dimly, be realized that the blast had hurled him against a flimsy door; the door had burst, and he lay inside a room. That frail door, serving to cushion his fall, had saved his life. A grim mockery stirred in his brain. It had spared his life, but perhaps only to be lost more terribly! Unless he could snap out of this awesome paralysis ....

Wentworth focused his powerful will on moving even a hand or foot—and failed! He concentrated on stirring a finger—the trigger finger of his right hand ... The sweat popped out on his face. The muscles of his face twitched. His whole body quivered with the effort to make that one finger move. The smoke was rolling more densely above his head, the crackle of the flames becoming a hollow, all-consuming roar. Lurid glare stained the smoke.

Mad thoughts danced through Wentworth's head, disjointed visions. He fought against them, pinned his will to its task. It seemed to him that faces jeered from the red depths of the fire-stained smoke—malignant, mocking faces. With this weapon of flame, they would devastate the land, dominate the people like terrified sheep. Not, by God, while the *Spider* lived! A shout of defiance inflated Wentworth's lungs. He coughed—and stirred. His finger moved ... then his hand, arm. Rapidly, he regained a fumbling control over his body, paralyzed by the explosion's shock. He got to his hands and knees. His shoulders were racked with pain as he crawled toward the window. It required an eternity of effort to get his head above the sill. The window was in the back—fortunate for the crippled *Spider!* Any man who found him now could kill him with impunity. A criminal would slaughter him on sight. The police hated the *Spider* with the vehemence of

defeated men. A hundred times he had
broken their laws—and slipped through
their fingers. What did it matter that he
sinned always in the name of justice?
That those he killed richly deserved
death? He had mocked and outwitted
them times without number and his life
was a hundred-fold forfeit to the courts.

Knowledge of all that flitted through
Wentworth's brain as he leaned heavily
on the windowsill, yet he could not pause

*The blast seemed to pick Wentworth
up and hurl him through space.*

to remove the disguise. The cape he could leave behind ... Fumblingly, he removed it and dug with still numbed fingers into its pocket for the silken line he carried there always, the rope which, scarcely larger than a lead pencil, would sustain a weight of seven hundred pounds. He looped it around a steam pipe, knotted an end beneath his arms and climbed laboriously to the sill. The smoke, the turbulent

heat of the fire thrust at him like living inimical hands. He twisted the line about one arm and swung out into space.

There was no strength in him to hold the silk, but the friction of the three loops about his arm held. It pulled his arm straight up over his head, and he curled his fingers to prevent the coils from ripping off. For twenty, thirty feet, he went down easily, then he fell. It could not have been more than ten feet, but he could not catch himself ....

It was many minutes before he could crawl, trailing the silken line behind him. Thought was no longer possible, only the tremendous will to live, to fight these new and overwhelming enemies of mankind. He did not even remember that the silken line was like none other in the world, that the police or criminals would recognize it on sight as the web of the *Spider*—that by it they would identify him ....

Vaguely, he heard voices, which held a peculiar sibilant quality that, for long moments, he could not place. Then he knew! They spoke in Spanish, as had those killers upstairs, hirelings of some strange master! Wentworth's head swung, but slowly. His eyes hunted desperately for a place to hide ....

CHAPTER THREE
Eyes of Fear

AS Wentworth had guessed, Nita van Sloan was prevented from rushing to his rescue when he had fought the knife-men out in front of the consulate. Don Carlos took a firm stand against the broad white door and his voice crackled with sharp orders to the staff while he held Nita back.

"I beg of you, señorita!" he cried. "Wait but a moment more. The servants are bringing revolvers. Without them, it would be madness to dash into the battle!"

Nita's eyes were a violet flame and scorn deepened her voice. "Will they know we are unarmed?" she cried. "Let them but see us charging out, and ... Ah, and the men of Spain are called *brave!*"

But Don Carlos could not be moved. Nita whirled from him, darted to a window and flung it up. She was in time to see Wentworth dashing for the Daimler and, moments later, start in pursuit. She sank to the floor with a cry of thankfulness on her lips and, seconds later, the door of the consulate flung wide. Don Carlos, with three men at his back, rushed out into the street and found it empty — save for the charred body of Martinez and the couple who had befriended Wentworth. With drawn guns, the consulate servants surrounded the two and herded them, protesting, into the building.

The man was young and his uncovered hair sprawled across his forehead. "You fools!" he shouted. "I'm not one of those gangsters! I was trying to help the guy! Listen, there's a wounded Hindu out there and the guy said to get him to the hospital right away. Look, he gave me his card."

Nita heard his young voice rising indignantly, and she pushed herself up from the sill where she knelt and came quickly out into the main foyer. For a moment, she stood watching them. The man had wrenched free of restraining hands and stood, at bay, an arm flung around the girl. His clothing was dust-marked, and she liked the way he stared his captors belligerently in the eyes, jaw set squarely. The girl was pale, but her head was up, too, bravely.

"You're a swell bunch!" the man said vehemently, "You let a guy get taken right in front of your door and don't do a damned thing until it's all over. You might at least get that Hindu to the hospital!"

Nita uttered a low cry. "It's Ram Singh, Don Carlos!" she said swiftly. "He must be hurt! I sent him to help Mr. Wentworth!"

Don Carlos gave a brief order, and two of the liveried footmen went out the front door.

Nita hurried forward. "This couple had nothing to do with the attack on Mr. Wentworth," she said curtly. "I saw them before the trouble started."

The man turned toward her, nodded his head. "Thanks, lady. I'll say I didn't have anything to do with it! I saw that guy go up in smoke, and then these three birds tried to knife another man. I found a gun on the sidewalk, and blazed away. I couldn't hit the side of a barn, but I made a noise anyhow, and they ran. I think I managed to wing one of them, at that. And then this guy ..." He looked at a calling-card, dirty now, which he held in his hand. *"Richard Wentworth,"* he read. "Well, Wentworth says let them go, and he hops in a car out front and chases them. He asks us to come and see him, didn't he, Beulah?"

Beulah nodded shortly. "Skip it, Miles," she said. "The lady doesn't need it, and these other mugs won't believe you. This Mr. Wentworth will straighten things out for us, and . . ." Her voice choked off abruptly, and she stared past Nita.

Beulah's eyes widened and she moved closer to the boy she called Miles. Nita turned deliberately and found that a man and woman stood in the doorway. The woman she recognized at once as Doña Margherita, the niece of the consul, but the man she had never seen before. He had a moon face and as he smiled and came forward apologetically, deep dimples pocked his cheeks.

Before he could speak, the front door swung wide and the two footmen struggled in with the limp weight of Ram Singh between them. Nita saw his turbaned head roll and, abruptly, the Sikh wrenched free of the men who carried him, sprang to his feet and, with a movement so swift his hand blurred, he snapped a long-bladed knife from its sheath in his sash.

"Friends, Ram Singh!" Nita cried out sharply and Ram Singh's bearded face swung toward her, his eyes narrow and hard.

"The *sahib!*" he demanded gutturally. "Where is the *sahib?*"

Nita explained rapidly. "Call Jackson to bring a car around," she ordered. "That is, if Don Carlos permits?" Her voice finished on a scornful note.

Don Carlos bowed low, smiling. "But of course, señorita—if you must leave! I had hoped you might remain."

Nita turned her shoulder on him and crossed to the two young people. "I cannot thank you enough," she told them quietly. "I hope you will go with me to Mr. Wentworth's home. He will count it an honor. I am Nita van Sloan, Mr. Wentworth's fiancée."

The man grinned and his face was suddenly boyish, very young, now that the anger had gone out of it. "That's swell of you," he said, "but I reckon I'd better get Beulah home before her folks romp all over me. It isn't far from here."

Nita smiled and held out her hand. "You know best, of course. But at least tell me your names and where you live. Mr. Wentworth will want to—"

Don Carlos interrupted smoothly, "I'm afraid you'll all have to wait for the police. I have had them called and they will have questions to ask about poor Martinez. His death was a horrible thing. That fire! Incredible, the speed with which it struck! And from no apparent source!"

"The police know where to find me," Nita said curtly.

"Look, I got to get Beulah home," the man said earnestly. "My name's Miles Scott, and I'll give you my address. Beulah here—Beulah Loraine, it is—lives around on Twenty-First street."

Don Carlos shrugged. "It is as you please, of course. I have no authority to interfere."

Miles Scott apologized to Nita and left hurriedly with Beulah.

NITA was forced to wait for the arrival of the car for which Ram Singh had phoned. Don Carlos did his best to restore social amenities. The moon-faced man he presented as Humboldt Tavish, and Nita inspected him curiously. There had been no mistaking Beulah's expression of fear when she had looked at the man. His name was vaguely familiar; it meant something in the financial world, as nearly as Nita could remember.

But she was too impatient to worry about it now. Dick Wentworth, somewhere in the city, was trailing three assassins. He was alone. Of course, Dick could look after himself, but that fire which had killed Martinez had struck so suddenly, so terribly! And Dick had hinted at some new terror creeping into this great city .... If she could have known where Wentworth was then, prostrate in a fire-swept tenement, stunned by the force of the blast of flame ....

It seemed incredible that Jackson should drive up to the door before the arrival of police, but he did, and Nita hurried with Ram Singh into the car. The Sikh's movements were stiff, rather uncertain, and Nita knew that his brain was still blurred by the concussion of the blast. But she was equally sure that he would feel disgraced if she dispatcbed him home as she should. NitA had no intention of returning to Wentworth's home yet. She was far too poignantly conscious of the danger which Dick might be facing.

"Tune the radio in on police broad-

RICHARD WENTWORTH

casts," she ordered curtly. "Ram Singh will explain something of what happened. The master is in pursuit with the Daimler. Drive toward the Spanish quarter on the Lower East Side."

In the years during which Wentworth had fought against the powers of the underworld, and Nita had fought beside him, she had acquired something of his own swift ability of analysis and intuitive suspicion. The fact that the police were so slow in arriving at the consulate was assuming larger proportions in her mind.

23

Don Carlos' earlier action in restraining her from dashing to help Dick was explicable, but the delay of the police could mean only one thing. They had not been called! The consulate was in a neighborhood which, in daytime, teemed with business people, but at night would be deserted except for the inhabitants of the consulate itself. Hence, any alarm must come from them ... and there was no such alarm!

The whine of the police station shrilled abruptly over the radio, then the voice of the announcer sending a car to Cherry Street.

"A large fire there of suspicious origin," the announcer droned. "Watch for suspicious persons."

Nita sat forward tensely, the words hammering in her brain. Cherry Street was in the heart of the Spanish quarter, She caught up the speaking-tube.

"Get to that fire fast," she ordered Jackson, and felt the surge as the powerful engine took hold. She tried to relax against the cushions as Wentworth had taught her to do in moments of tension. It helped the brain to work swiftly, prepared her more alertly for action, but her heart beat fast and violently. She *knew* that something had gone wrong; Dick was in danger.

Nita van Sloan made a lovely picture, apparently at ease in the rear of that rich car, her proud head with its crisp crown of chestnut curls held bravely erect, her features expressing a chiseled calm. More than one person turned to gaze enviously at her as the powerful motor whirled her rapidly through the streets.

Once Nita leaned forward to snap open a compartment in the rear of the front seat and take out two heavy automatics that dwarfed her slender, exquisite hands. But there was no uncertainty in the way she handled them, checking the loading, jacking a cartridge into the chamber and thumbing on the safety. This, too, she had learned from Dick, at his insistence, when she had demanded the right to share the danger of his life.

Once more, she leaned back and tried to relax with those heavy guns in her fists. Nita had no quarrel with her lot. She had entered this life—the secret life of the *Spider*—with wide-open eyes. And if sometimes she gazed wistfully on the quiet home life of others, she did not complain. She knew how Dick had fought against the love that had been stronger than even his mighty will. But in the end, it had been Nita who had spoken, guessing that some secret held the man she loved from the future for which they both longed. And so she had learned the secret of the *Spider,* of Wentworth's honor which would not let him marry while there hung hourly over his head the threat of disgrace and death. If ever the time should come when the police and the laws of the nation could keep down the savage forces of crime, they would be married, but until that time ....

Nita sighed and thrust the thought from her, bent forward eagerly as a fresh announcement came over the radio dispatching a car to the Spanish consulate. "Signal thirty," the announcement concluded, meaning, as Nita knew, a crime of violence had been committed there. She frowned. There was no longer any doubt in her mind. Don Carlos was somehow involved in the death of his assistant, Martinez!

THE abrupt application of brakes jerked Nita almost to the floor. She sprang erect, guns in hand. "What's the matter, Jackson?" she demanded sharply.

"The major's car!" Jackson cried.

"I'm sure it was parked in that last street we passed!"

Already he had the car in reverse, was snaking it backward along the street. Nita waited while he jumped out and ran toward the parked Daimler, came hurriedly back.

"It's the Daimler, all right!" Jackson said crisply, and muscles were working along his broad jaws. "The left front door and window have been peppered with bullets. But none of them got through."

"Get to that fire fast!" Nita ordered. "It's only a few blocks from here!"

Jackson saluted and sprang behind the wheel, slammed the car forward. Nita could see anxiety in the square forward thrust of his shoulders. His loyalty to Wentworth was scarcely second to her own. They had fought through the war together, sergeant and major, and Jackson still used the war-time title to refer to his master; giving him the same un-questioning, unswerving faithfulness that had been his on the battlefields. The car flashed across Cherry Street, took the next parallel behind the blazing tenement.

"The major may be in that building," Nita called sharply as Jackson braked to a halt. "Get into the court behind it. Ram Singh ..." She had been on the point of ordering him to remain with the car, but a glimpse of his set face told her that would be too great a trial on his love for the *sahib*. "Go with Jackson!" she commanded. She sprang to the pavement.

"You're staying here, Miss Nita," Jackson said, almost pleadingly.

Nita did not bother to answer. With guns gripped hard in her fists beneath her opera cloak, she raced along a sidestreet toward the fire-lines, found an alley-way that led into the back-courts and dashed through with Jackson and Ram Singh at her heels. Abruptly, she flung up a hand in an order to halt. The whisper of voices that she had heard was louder now, and she caught the sibilance of Spanish.

"It is of no use to try to get him to the master," a man was saying. "The police would stop us. Cut his throat and let us fly! We will take his head as proof !"

Breath gasped from Nita's throat. She *knew*—that somewhere in the darkness ahead, men were preparing to kill . . . Richard Wentworth! And it would be impossible for her to locate them before a keen-edged knife. With something very like a prayer, Nita flung up an automatic and fired into the darkness toward the sound of those voices. She fired high, lest her bullets find the wrong target—spaced shots that sledged through the night with a crash like dynamite bombs. She shouted in a deliberately deepened voice.

"Close in!" she cried. "Close in. Surrender, you fools, before we blow you to bits!" Then she repeated the order in Spanish. There was a sob in her throat as she finished, and Jackson and Ram Singh darted past her like eager dogs. She ran after them swiftly, still firing as she went, straight upward into the night now. The first gun clicked empty and she began to blast with the second.

In the darkness ahead, she heard Jackson's short, challenging shout, Ram Singh's guttural battle-cry. Vaguely now, she could see struggling shapes. Her breath came pantingly. Dear God, had she been too late? Had she succeeded in scaring those assassins before .... She could not finish the thought. They were directly behind the burning building now and a dancing red light threw contorted shadows on the ground. But there was one shadow that did not move, one shadow ....

Nita flung herself to her knees beside it, pillowed Wentworth's head in her lap and felt him feebly stir. Nita twined her arms about him, and the sobs came.

"Oh, Dick, Dick!" she whispered. She laughed a little, wildly. "Thank heavens, you made me learn Spanish!"

But Wentworth was trying to get words across. He thrust against the ground. "My disguise!" His voice was no more than a whisper. "The *Spider* disguise ...."

Nita's fingers brushed his face, lightly as down. And, in the darkness, she set swiftly to work. Other feet were pounding in the darkness, men shouting.

"Warn them, Jackson!" Nita cried. "It's the police! Tell them who we are before .... "

"This way!" Jackson shouted. "Police, this way! This is Richard Wentworth! I have some prisoners for you!"

Wentworth laughed faintly, and Nita laughed, too, in relief. She knew that tears were streaming down her cheeks and did not care. The last fragments of the disguise which she could remove were torn off now. The taut texture of the skin she could not change without proper chemicals, but she smeared her fingers in dirt and smudged Dick's face.

"Now," he said, "you can untie me. Those men stumbled on me when I was crawling away from the fire, recognized me as the *Spider.* From what they said, the man they call the 'Master' has offered a big reward for my... my head."

Nita shuddered. "I know. I heard them."

Police lights stabbed at them in the darkness. Jackson and Ram Singh stood over two prostrate bodies on the ground, and Jackson was grinning.

"I thought we had some prisoners here," he said, "but it looks to me as though they'd go better in the morgue than in jail."

A man stood over Wentworth, the light streaming down upon him. "Gee, Mr. Wentworth," he said, "they kind of messed you up, didn't they? They ..." His voice broke off and when he spoke it was harsh. "How come, Mr. Wentworth," he asked flatly, "that you got some of the *Spider's* web wrapped around you?"

CHAPTER FOUR
The Flaming Horde

INSTANT hostility had sprung into the policeman's voice. His gun hand stiffened, and Nita bit her lips in anxiety. She had stripped off the disguise, but the obvious silken line she had overlooked, and now ....

Wentworth's voice was weak, "Don't be an ass, Sergeant Reams," he said. "The *Spider* saved my life when the smoke knocked me out in the building. He lowered me out of the window with his web."

Reams crouched forward, stared down into Wentworth's face, and Nita felt tension creep over her. Both her guns were on the ground there beside Dick, empty. Suppose Reams should not believe Dick? Suppose he should detect the remnants of the disguise.

"Swear to that!" Reams demanded harshly.

Wentworth said, "Of course. Now, get me to Commissioner Kirkpatrlck as soon as possible. Hell's going to pop in this city."

He called to his two faithful servitors and with their help began to walk along the dark alleyway by which Nita had entered. He was still light-headed and his feet fumbled for the ground, but his marvelous recuperative powers already were at work. His brain was clear, and he had Nita rapidly tell him what had occurred in the consulate.

"Humboldt Tavish!" he echoed the

man's name. "Jackson, I can get along now. Skip over to the addresses Miss Nita will give you, take Miss Beulah Loraine and Miles Scott to my home. They are friends. And I think—I am very sure they are in danger."

Even in the darkness of the street, Wentworth spotted Kirkpatrick a half block away. Even if he had not been beside the headquarters' sedan, that ramrod erectness, that stiff poise of the head would have identified him. When he saw Wentworth, he hurried forward.

"What's up, Dick?" he asked crisply. "What are you doing down here?" Belatedly he bowed to Nita, but his frowning attention swung instantly back to Wentworth's face. "You've been hurt!"

Wentworth smiled, "Just knocked about a bit," he explained. "Why does the commissioner of police find it necessary to come to a tenement fire? Or is there more in this than meets the eye?"

Kirkpatrick's smile was dour on his saturnine face, "Suppose you tell me, Wentworth," he said quietly, "and don't forget to fill in the part about Martinez at the Spanish Consulate. As for my presence, Martinez' death, as it was described, seemed almost incredible. Coming on top of it, this tenement fire that spread like a gasoline blaze aroused my curiosity. That's all."

Wentworth said grimly, "Kirk, the underworld is going to war again, with a weapon of fire we have no means to fight. We've got to strike quickly, or it will be too late."

For moments, Kirkpatrick's frosty blue gaze held on his face, then he turned crisply. "Get in my car, Dick. Nita? I was afraid of this."

Wentworth moved slowly to the car and climbed into the back rather laboriously. His brain was skimming over the events of the night, trying to pick out those that were important. Commissioner Kirkpatrick would listen to him, probably. Their relations were rather peculiar. Close friends, they had begun as enemies when suspicion had first pointed to Richard Wentworth as the *Spider.* They lived now in a species of armed truce. If Kirkpatrick ever found absolute and unmistakable proof of his suspicions, Wentworth knew that he could expect no mercy. But until that time came, they were stout friends and allies against the powers of the underworld. Kirkpatrick respected Wentworth's judgment, invited his help as he did now. Seated in the car, he turned to Wentworth.

"This weapon, what is it?" he asked. "Who's behind it?"

Wentworth had only begun to talk when the radio, tuned always to police headquarters, whined as the carrying wave came in. The announcer's voice held the snap and crackle of tension.

"Cars Two-three-five, Eighty-nine, Detective Cruiser Nineteen, make all speed to Fifth Avenue and Fiftieth Street. Fire and robbery. Criminals dangerous, armed .... "

Kirkpatrick's voice cut in harshly. "Mac, get this car rolling. North on Fifth Avenue. And make it fast!"

The chauffeur sprang to the wheel and instantly the heavy limousine was under way. The siren purred, rose to a shriek that burst eerily through the night. Above its fury, Kirkpatriek's crisp voice was audible.

"I'm afraid you are right, Dick!" Without a word, Nita laid the two automatics she had been carrying in Wentworth's lap. "They're empty, Dick," she said quietly.

Silently, Kirkpatrick produced a box of ammunition from a compartment, and

Wentworth began to stuff bullets into the clips. He lifted his voice above the bedlam of their race northward.

"I really know very little about this flame," he said. "I know that each time there was an odor of ozone in the air, that some gas—probably an overabundance of oxygen—is present in sufficient quantities to intoxicate any person that breathes it. Each time, it was a pistolshot that set off the flames. The explosive force is not tremendous. All explosions, of course, are merely incredibly rapid combustion with an accompanying expansion of gases. I think the combustion rate in this case is between that of gasoline and kerosene. There's only one thing I can't understand. It seemed to me that *Martinez' flesh was on fire.* Exactly as if human flesh were a combustible material. Sorry, Nita dear. Perhaps you'd better not listen."

Nita's face was dead white, not with the shock of what she had heard, but with the thought of Dick fighting against criminals who could loose such a weapon. If they turned it on Dick... She shuddered and felt Dick's arm close about her shoulders.

KIRKPATRICK leaned forward and caught up the small microphone, his car being equipped with two-way radio. Number One calling headquarters," he said quietly. "Number One calling headquarters. Send two emergency wagons to Fifth Avenue fire and robbery. All men to put on asbestos suits. Number One on way to fire. Come back, headquarters."

He closed the circuit and a moment later got his acknowledgment from headquarters. Wentworth was lolling back, gathering his strength for the battle he knew lay ahead, but there was a coldness around his heart that would not let him rest. Other men would reach the scene far ahead of them, brave police who would rush into the battle with drawn guns—and die as living torches! Unless ... Wentworth lifted his head and voiced his fears to Kirkpatrick.

"Warn all men not in asbestos suits to hold back, to throw a cordon around the place and shoot on sight," he urged. "There's no use in sacrificing lives needlessly. We don't know the full potentialities of this new weapon. I'm positive of that."

Kirkpatrick agreed crisply and relayed the order to headquarters, also calling to the cars which were racing for the scene. It was sometimes possible to communicate directly with other cars, though reception in the city was spotty and erratic. Kirkpatrick sat stiffly forward, his eyes boring ahead into the night. The red glow of the fire shone against the sky.

"Lord," Kirkpatrick whispered, "It's a conflagration! It looks to me..."

"Headquarters calling Number One," the radio cut in. "Three alarms have been hit on the Fifth Avenue fire."

Kirkpatrick's lips snapped shut. His fist beat his knee, but Wentworth forced himself to relax. Ahead of them, an emergency wagon swung into Fifth Avenue and, with bellowing siren, roared up the street. Kirkpatrick's limousine slashed past and Wentworth had a brief glimpse of the men in the open wagon struggling into asbestos armor. His own jaw set grimly. He had a premonition of overwhelming disaster. Kirkpatrick had not seen the fury of those flames. If human flesh would burn, would asbestos stand against their attack?

Abruptly, he leaned forward in his seat, too. The fire was within sight. At first glimpse, he knew that there had never before been such a blaze as this in New York—in the world! The corner building was built of stone and steel. Usually, in such a structure, the flames gutted the interior, flapped out of windows. If the walls fell, it was from internal heat and the collapse of supports. But in this fire ... the *stones themselves were burning!*

WENTWORTH stared incredulously, turned to find Kirkpatrick's horror-widened eyes on his own, felt Nita's hand tight on his arm. Firemen in asbestos garments crouched behind shields in an attempt to brave that awful heat and reach the flames with water that changed to steam almost before it struck!

As they raced nearer, a fire truck swung wildly away from the fire zone and raced toward them and, even as it fled, flames burst out beneath it, swept over it and, in one vast enveloping explosion, engulfed the entire piece of equipment. A man's high, tearing scream wailed to them out of the night. And the truck was running wild down the street!

With a wrench that almost capsized the limousine, Kirkpatrick's driver skidded into a sidestreet, as the blazing truck raced past. Wentworth saw the flaming Juggernaut leap high as it sprang across the curb and heard the crash as it slammed into a store window. An instant later, a shattering explosion drove in the windows of the limousine, popped them into glittering shards. For half a block, Kirkpatrick's car reeled crazily as the chauffeur fought the effects of the concussion. His brakes howled, and he jerked the lumbering car to a halt within inches of a lamp post, slumped forward over the wheel.

Kirkpatrick sprang to the street, but Wentworth hauled him back and climbed behind the wheel of the car.

"That was an accident," he called, and his voice sounded dull and flat in his own ears.

Kirkpatrick swore at him raggedly, "Accident? Accident?"

Wentworth had the car rolling, throwing words back over his shoulder. "We can't help here! Up there, near the fire somewhere, are the men who started it! They had a reason. Robbery. When we find the reason, we'll find the men."

Kirkpatrick crouched behind the seat, keeping his feet, holding on as Wentworth swung the corner in a squealing skid. Wentworth knew that his head still spun from the blast, that he was scarcely speaking lucidly, but his idea was clear. This destruction was beyond checking now, but the operations of the fiends behind this horror had just begun. As useless to fight the fire as to apply salve to small-pox sores. They must find the seat of the infection, wipe it out. As he flashed past the corner of the next cross-street, the heart of the conflagration struck like a sledge. They were past in a moment, but Wentworth found himself gasping for breath. Rage burned through his veins. In heaven's name, how could any human beings loose such a fearful thing upon mankind! Human beings? They were fiends out of hell!

Wentworth had known that he had not guessed half of the horror that threatened, but even in his wildest fears, he had pictured no such weapon as this—a weapon that even the masters of modern warfare shrank from using! Three blocks beyond the point of the fire, Wentworth whirled the car westward again, braked to a halt. Fifth Avenue was choked with fire-fighting equipment and police. Wentworth twisted about in his seat and the white, contorted face of Kirkpatrick stared back at him.

"Dynamite," Wentworth said curtly. "That's the only thing that can possibly stop the spread of that fire. I don't know whether even that will suffice. If you can get hold of the fire chief ..." He sprang to the ground. "Nita, will you try to revive this chauffeur? Then stick by the radio."

Kirkpatrick was beside him on the pavement. "We can trust the fire chief to use dynamite, I think. You have an idea where we can find these ... these fiends?"

"Two banks in that block where the fire started," Wentworth snapped. "That must be what they're after."

For a moment, Wentworth hesitated beside the car, gazing into Nita's eyes. "If you'd only go home, where you'd be reasonably safe ..." He saw the uselessness of pushing the request.

Nita leaned toward him a moment, touched her lips to his, then smiled. She said nothing. Wentworth pivoted on his heel and began to run, Kirkpatrick beside him, toward Madison Avenue. At the corner, they found a policeman stationed, and Kirkpatrick flung a swift question, as they raced on. Wentworth had not even hesitated. It had been no more than fifteen minutes since the first alarm. Unless the crooks had been secretly working long before that, there was small chance that they had yet finished the looting of the banks. His mind was racing, trying to anticipate the strategy of the looters.

THEY could see the flames licking up into the night sky now and heat was beginning to beat at them. It was plain that the fire had now spread to several buildings along Fifth Avenue and along Fifty-first Street. Firemen were working in Fifty-second, sheltered from the fire by the walls of buildings, and even there they were falling out like flies. A constant stream of stretchers carried the overcome men to waiting ambulances. Half way to Fifty-second Street, Wentworth pulled to a halt. He was panting, his heart hammering from exertion and yet—and yet he felt a strange lift to his senses, as if he had found a new source of boundless strength. He gasped a curse, sniffing the air with distended nostrils, swung to Kirkpatrick.

"Get these men out of here!" he gasped. "Get every man out of this area in the next few minutes, or it will be too late!"

Kirkpatrick stared at him, "Are you crazy?" he demanded harshly. "They've got to check that fire!"

"Unless they're out within the next few minutes," Wentworth said violently, "every one of them will be dead. Every one of them will be burning alive! Damn it, Kirk, can't you smell . . . *the ozone!* The crooks are getting ready for a crush-out, and they're going to come out behind a veil of fire. They're filling this area with that damnable gas, chemical, whatever it is, and when they touch it off, every man in it will burst into flames!"

Kirkpatrick stood rigidly, his eyes questing over the street. "You're sure, Dick?" he cried. "Oh, hell, of course you are... Chief Dogan! *Chief Dogan!*"

He raced toward a man who stood on the hood of a car, shouting directions to the firemen. Wentworth stared after him for a moment, then ran in his wake. He knew Chief Dogan, a good firefighter, but a stubborn, hard-headed man. There wasn't a chance . . . He sprang to a fire truck parked in the street, found a fire helmet and rubber coat, and threw them on. Kirkpatrick was shouting up at Dogan, who yelled back angrily, waving his arms. Wentworth ran up beside Kirkpatrick.

"Orders from Chief Donavan!" he bellowed up at Dogan. "Get all your men out! Dynamiters are coming! Donavan says be out in two minutes!"

Without waiting to see the result of his cry, Wentworth pivoted on his heel and ran back the way he had come. Moments later, Kirkpatrick overtook him, caught him by the shoulder.

"Tell Chief Donavan ..." he began, then swore. "You, Dick!"

Wentworth pulled him behind the truck, shed fire hat and coat while he talked. "You can't argue with Dogan, you ought to know that," he snapped. "Listen!"

Dogan's hoarse voice was bellowing orders, and already men were beginning to stream out of the area. Kirkpatrick smiled grimly. "All right, it worked. Now what?"

Wentworth's eyes were flashing over the scene. "If you can get a squad of men, Kirk, with machine guns on the roofs of the buildings up near the corner of Fifty-third, they should be safe enough. Block the streets that stem out of here, with trucks and autos. Then when the beasts behind this thing try to crush out ...."

Kirkpatrick jerked a curt nod. "You're sure, Dick?" he asked again. Wentworth swore at him, "For God's sake, hurry, Kirk! I don't know how much time we have, but it can't be much. That ozone is getting stronger every moment!"

"I'll use the radio in my car," Kirkpatrick snapped, and sprinted back the way they had come.

Wentworth moved to the sidewalk, watching the men staggering out of Fifty-second, hearing Dogan's hoarse shouts. Would they be in time? Wentworth ached to spring into the work, but it would be worse than useless. If he attempted to warn Dogan of the true danger... Two minutes, he had allowed Dogan. An impossible task, but they were moving. They were *moving*.

Wentworth's hands brushed the automatics in his belt, patted the box of ammunition in his pocket and his eyes went up to the roofs. When the blast of death and flames he was sure impended cut loose, its heat would surge upward. If he went above the danger line, his guns would be at too long range for effective, fast work. He ... Wentworth's face grew grim with determination. In two strides, he had reached one of the fire trucks, and after a few moment's search found what he wanted—a manhole key!

No one paid any attention to him, one hurrying figure among so many. He knew it was a desperate chance he took. The scent of the ozone was powerful now, even through the acrid odor of burning. He felt its elation pumping in his veins. A fireman he passed was staggering, laughing crazily. Another was bawling a scrap of off-key song. Dogan wavered where he stood on top of the hood of the car. Something like hysterical laughter pushed up into Wentworth's throat, but he fought it down. God, the time must be perilously short now!

HE staggered out into the street toward a manhole, bent over it with the long iron key. His hands seemed to have no control over the thing, and the impulse to laughter would not be held down. The sounds pushed out of his throat like dry sobs. He bent forward more intently and almost lurched forward on his face. Wentworth held his breath, and it steadied him a little. At last he threw the bolts that held the manhole enver in place. He inserted the hook of the key and put all his strength into a quick heave. At last!

Laughing crazily, Wentworth plunged into the hole, clinging to the rungs of the iron ladder, teetered the manhole cover back into its socket above him. In the close bricked-in cell where he stood, the air was foul, but Wentworth sucked it in with thankfulness, breathing fast, pumping the overdose of oxygen out of his lungs, out of his blood. He was dizzy with it. He ... The manhole jarred in its socket and the enclosed air beat heavily against Wentworth's eardrums. Flame spurted down through the small openings in the manhole cover and licked at his face, then sucked back. But that was all—all was safety here in the manhole. Up above, men were screaming, and there was the deep, hollow roar of flames!

Wentworth lifted one automatic into view and squeezed the trigger.

CHAPTER FIVE
Coming of the Flame-men

HOW long the flames roared over-head, Wentworth did not know. They swept the street like living hell even after the screams of the men had died. Inside his close-pressing prison, the heat was in-tense, and presently the man hole cover began to glow red. Wentworth shrank away from it, crawling down into the deeper recesses of this man-made cavern. Rage possessed him. He was restless with the need for action, for striking at the

criminals behind this massacre by torture. He kept his eyes on that heat-reddened cover of iron and when its brilliance began to fade, he climbed rapidly up the ladder again.

The roar of the flames was gone, and Wentworth went feverishly to work. Bracing the long iron key against the cover, he levered it up, sliding it to one side, so that once more he could gaze up into the vault of the night. But there was no dark sky this night. It was streaked with the crimson, hot-orange and yellow of flame! Wentworth eased his head above the level of the ground and a curse grated out between his teeth. He was in time! He laughed harshly—and it was the flat and mocking mirth of the *Spider* that issued from his lips.

What he had glimpsed was the hood of an automobile thrusting out of Fifty-second Street into Madison and swinging toward the manhole where he crouched. The laughter died on his lips. For men walked beside the auto ... but such men as Wentworth had never seen before!

From head to foot, they were garbed in scarlet; over their heads were hoods of the same color. That much of them was human, though bizarre. But, God in heaven, how could human beings walk—*clothed in flame!* For a moment, Wentworth thought the appearance was some illusion that his eyes had created out of glare and horror. Then he knew he could not be mistaken. Those men, from head to foot, glittered with living points of fire! The flames flickered about their striding legs, wrapped about their bodies, rose to flapping tongues and spires above their heads! Even as he stared, one of the men apparently spotted him, for a machine gun was lifted and began to hose bullets at his half exposed head!

Once more, Wentworth laughed. They were human enough! Heaven alone knew what trickery lay behind that clothing of flame, or what purpose it served, but only human beings used guns. And it was a leaden language, that Wentworth could answer! While bullets plowed the heat-melted asphalt near his head, he lifted one automatic into view and squeezed the trigger. The man with the machine gun toppled forward as if a sledge-hammer had struck him in the back. His gun flew high, and he pitched on his face in the street!

The automobile swerved around the corner, pointed straight for the manhole where Wentworth crouched. The engine's roar deepened. Behind it, a second and then a third machine bellowed. The men inside the cars wept garbed in scarlet, too, but no flames danced about them. Only those who ran beside the cars, pouring bullet streams at Wentworth, were clothed in fire. Wentworth was completely protected from bullets, up to his eyes. Running men could not shoot accurately enough to hit the small target of his head. And he was waiting, until he could make every bullet count. He strained his ears for other guns that might be backing his own. Had Kirkpatrick had time to post his men on the roofs? Could they have survived the fierce rising heat of the flames as he had? An agony of apprehension shook Wentworth. God, had he sent Kirkpatrick to his death...?

WENTWORTH'S lips shut in a thin, uncompromising line. He began to shoot with the slow assurance of target practice. His first bullet he lined on the first car's driver. He saw the glass frost where his gun had fired, but the car drilled straight on. Bulletproof glass! With a curse, Wentworth changed his aim, hammered a slug into the left front tire. Instantly, the car swerved wildly. Two of the flaming men were in its path, and Wentworth smiled grimly as they went down, screaming, before its charge. His second bullet took the gasoline tank from end to end and an instant later, it burst with a shattering blast.

The rear of that car leaped a yard into the air, slued around and crashed against the building wall. Gouts of liquid flame sprayed over its body, spread in a pool beneath the car itself, and men spilled from its open doors, their guns blasting.

But the other two cars were within thirty feet of Wentworth now, drilling toward him with fiercely mounting speed... Wentworth snapped a bullet at the tires of the first, missed and ducked so violently he lost his hold and dropped five feet before he caught himself. The tire of the charging car jounced across the hole and Wentworth flung himself upward again.

A moment later, and that wheel would have driven his head against the side wall, crushed it like an egg. But he had to get back up there fast. Once let any one of those killers reach the mouth of the hole, and he was doomed! A burst of machine-gun slugs could not miss him. Even an automatic would probably finish him off. In the narrow confines, there could be no dodging. While he was still a foot below the top, the second automobile roared overhead. Wentworth flung a bullet upward, but there was no chance to see what he had accomplished. He thrust gun and head over the edge—and a hand-grenade struck the pavement within inches of his face, wobbled toward the lip of the hole!

Wentworth acted almost without thought. He ducked down, and in the same instant, sent a .45 caliber slug at the grenade. Instantly, there was a terrific blast. Fragments of the grenade screamed overhead. Stunned by the concussion, Wentworth felt his hands loosening their hold on the ladder, felt his body sagging. Numbly, he pointed his automatic upward and began to pump bullets toward the sky. While that lasted no man would dare approach, but if they threw another grenade now ....

Dizzily, he fought for his senses, struggled upward. A machine gun was hammering, and a slug, catching the lip of the hole, ricocheted downward, rang tinnily on the iron ladder. Wentworth's auto-matic clicked emptily and he thrust it away, drew the other weapon. There was a lull in the storm of bullets and he thrust his head into sight.

Ten feet away, a man in scarlet was crawling forward with a machine gun. Wentworth ducked back and waited, his lips set grimly. He heard feet rasp on the pavement, thrust his hand above the edge and fired. He heard the man's muffled scream, clatter of the falling gun. He thrust above the edge again.

His bullet had smashed the scarlet man's leg. The machine gun lay within arm's length of the manhole. Other guns were hammering now, the body of the fallen man jerking with the hammer of slugs as he was mercilessly sacrificed to the necessity of killing Wentworth. The betrayed man's screams stopped, but Wentworth laughed aloud. He had the machine gun—and there were more au-tomobiles streaming from the cross-street. As the first raced toward him, the flames which had clothed the foot sol-diery of the fire, winked out. They leaped to the running-boards, some springing inside.

They might have spared themselves the effort. Wentworth had a weapon to his liking now, and there was death in the fierce gleam of his blue-grey eyes. His first burst smashed through the wind-shield of the car. As he had guessed, only those first few which carried the leaders, and probably the loot, were armored.

The car whipped in a tight turn, tee-tered on two wheels, and smashed over on its side. Wentworth sewed a seam along its roof, then swung the machine gun's muzzle in a slow arc across the street. Bullets hummed about his ears like a swarm of bees, but only for fractions of a second. Then his machine gun complet-ed its arc and there was silence on the street—silence save for the groans of the wounded and dying ...

BEHIND him, Wentworth could now hear the hammer of other guns, and he knew that Kirkpatrick's machine gunners were at work. For the moment, the Spider's task was done. But the skies still blazed with crimson and, now that the heat of battle was over, Wentworth felt the assault of the flames. Dazedly, he crawled from the manhole and staggered along the street.

One of the scarlet-clad figures lay in his path and, for a moment, he stood above it, staring with narrowed eyes. Fury ate at him. With a curse, he drove a kick at the corpse. He tried to lift the body to his shoulder. Failing in that, he sought to rip the scarlet uniform away. There was a chance that he might identify the man. At least, he could learn the secret of those flames ....

A shout reached his ears, and he lifted his head to see Nita running toward him along the deserted street. "Run!" she cried. "They're dynamiting! Run .... "

With a curse, Wentworth sprang to his feet and raced toward her. He motioned frantically for her to turn and retreat, but she waited for him to come. Hand in hand then, they fled up the street where the bodies of scarlet-clad men and the burned corpses of their victims littered the pavement. His keen eyes, sweeping the way ahead, failed to find any more of the cars of the criminals. They had got away!

"Around this corner!" Nita gasped, and Wentworth swung beside her. An instant later, there was a series of rumbling explosions, and Nita slowed to a walk. Wentworth staggered and braced a hand against the wall, stood panting for a moment. He smiled faintly into Nita's anxious eyes.

"Kirkpatrick?" he asked anxiously. "He's at the car," Nita panted. "He's organizing the pursuit. Oh, Dick, those flames! I thought .. . you were dead!"

Wentworth pushed out from the wall and threw an arm around Nita's shoulders, turning her toward Kirkpatrick's car as he hurried on again. "It was close," he admitted. "Close! We've got to work fast! With such a weapon as this, the criminals will have the city at their mercy! The city?" he repeated. "They'll have the world!"

HE COULD hear Kirkpatrick's voice, speaking crisply into the microphone, even before they reached the car. He was weaving a cordon around the city to prevent the escape of the fleeing cars; blocking streets with trucks, trying to trap the killers. Wentworth stood at the door, and Kirkpatrick's eyes whipped about. He broke off for a moment in his swift orders, and the relaxation of relief worked a miracle in his taut face.

"Thank God, Dick!" he said simply, and turned back to his task. He closed the circuit to see if there were any reports for him from headquarters.

"I have a report for Number One," the announcer droned. "Police located the homes of man and woman ordered picked up —Miles Scott and Beulah Loraine. They were not found. Signal seventeen. End report." The voice ran on, acknowledging other orders, reporting on the progress of blockades. Kirkpatrick listened with half an ear, facing Wentworth.

"I want those youngsters, Scott and the girl," he said. "We've got to have their report. It may give us some information about the men behind this thing."

Wentworth nodded curtly. "They are at my home—I hope. I sent Jackson and Ram Singh after them hours ago. If they knew anything, they were in danger. At the Spanish consulate, their names and addresses were known."

Kirkpatrick nodded. "We'll go there at once then," he said shortly. "Afterward, we'll pay a visit to the consulate. I've got a dozen men watching it now. If any one attempts to go in or out. they'll be taken into custody. God, that was an awful thing, Dick—those brave men snuffed out in flames!" He shook his clenched fist. "By the heavens, when I get these fiends into my clutches ..."

Wentworth nodded, his own face strained and hard. "I hope you don't, Kirk," he said softly. "I hope I find them first. Legal processes are often slow."

Kirkpatrick stared at him, and slowly a grim smile crept across his drawn face. "I think I can promise that the legal processes I employ won't be... too slow, Dick," he said flatly.

The big limousine gathered speed and turned eastward toward Wentworth's new riverside home. The radio shrilled with the police signal again and the announcer's crisp voice cut through swiftly.

"Number One, I have a special message from the home of Richard Wentworth," he rattled off. "Report from Jackson. Mission failed. Man was missing. Report from Ram Singh. Mission failed. Wounded in pursuit. Condition not critical. That is all."

Nita uttered a little cry, caught Wentworth's arm. He pressed back a curse that sprang to his lips. "Ram Singh wounded!" he cried. "That means the girl was kidnapped—or killed! He went after Beulah Loraine! I was right then, but too late. Those two youngsters hold a key to this hellish thing, but the criminals got to them first. They have been seized by . . . the 'master'!"

"The master?" Kirkpatrick repeated blankly.

Wentworth's grin was savage. "They call him that... 'the Master of the Flaming Hordes'! How long have your men been on the watch at the consulate?"

Kirkpatrick stared thoughtfully at Wentworth. "The order was issued less than a half hour ago. We should have thought of it sooner. I should have."

Wentworth made no answer. He was sitting back against the cushions again, frowning heavily. "Several things are queer at the consulate," he said slowly, "but I'd like to talk to Ram Singh before we go there."

He then detailed that Martinez had reported Don Carlos frightened at the prospect of Wentworth's visit; that Nita had virtually been held prisoner within the consulate; that the telephone call to the police had been delayed until the two, Miles Scott and Beulah Loraine, had left; that some of the enemy definitely were Spanish.

"Of course, it's possible that there were others of the crew in the neighborhood," Wentworth said, "at the time of the attack on me, and that these followed Scott and the girl home. On the other hand, I was not followed when I pursued the assassins, so I doubt that Don Carlos heard them give their address to Nita; so did other occupants of the consulate; so did Humboldt Tavish."

"Tavish?" Kirkpatrick interrupted sharply. "No mention of him was made in my report on the case."

Wentworth shrugged. "He's paying court to Doña Margherita, the consul's niece. He *may* have merely wanted to avoid publicity."

"He may," Kirkpatrick acknowledged grimly.

The limousine was flashing across Sutton Place into a dead-end street that ended in an embankment slanting steeply to the East River. On their left was a high, smooth white wall. As the car swung toward it, a gate parted and slid silently aside and when the car flashed through, it shut with a heavy thud of steel. Jackson stepped from a small cubicle just inside the wall, saluted.

"Doctor Griggs is with Ram Singh, Major," he reported briefly. "Got a ball through the groin. It tore the lumbar muscle, but the doctor says it isn't serious unless complications develop."

"Good." Wentworth's worry was apparent in his relief. "I was afraid that 'not critical' was Ram Singh's own idea. He wouldn't think anything less than decapitation was serious."

"He has courage," Kirkpatrick acknowledged curtly. "Can he talk?"

Jackson's grin was admiring. "He can. Wouldn't take an anesthetic while the doctor went after the bullet. Said the *sahib* would want his story."

THEY hurried into the new four-story building which Wentworth had erected, partly on filled ground between two piers that jutted into the East River. The place was as nearly impregnable against assault as Wentworth's ingenuity and modern science could make it. Before this, criminal cohorts had laid siege to his home ....

They hurried in through a wide hallway in whose walls were masked gun-slits, entered an elevator which shot them to the third story. Nita's hand rested lightly on Wentworth's arm. She knew the tenderness beneath this hard exterior, knew his concern over Ram Singh and his grief that the man should have taken injury in his service. Not that Ram Singh counted any cost except the fact that for a few days he would be unable to serve the *sahib* he worshiped.

Doctor Grigg was just leaving Ram Singh's room. He glowered at Wentworth, crushed a hand across his bristly mop of red hair without subduing it in the least. "One of these times," he said grimly, "I'm not going to be able to patch up these war-dogs of yours, Dick, but I've laid Ram Singh up for a while this time. If he navigates in less than a month with that torn lumbar, he'll have to get a concrete cast. And I won't make one." He shook his head at the question in Wentworth's eyes. "It'll take more than one bullet to put that beggar on the danger list, but make your questions short."

"*Wah!*" Ram Singh's deep voice rolled scornfully, but weakly from the room. "It is a flea-bite. Thy servant is an old woman."

Wentworth stepped quickly inside, peered down into the Sikh's bearded face. His forehead was sweat-dabbled, but his teeth showed white in a smile.

"Tell me, warrior," Wentworth

dropped into a chair and lapsed into Punjabi, Ram Singh's native tongue.

Ram Singh closed his eyes. "Obeying thy orders, master, thy servant went to the house of the woman. As he entered the building, a rat bit him in the back. When this rat slunk nearer, thy servant's knife was ready, and he died. Then men who looked like demons, in scarlet clothes and with scarlet hoods over their heads, carried an unconscious woman from the building. One of them struck thy servant, and this weak one lost consciousness. That is all, master."

Wentworth nodded curtly. "What could be done, thou hast done, my warrior," Wentworth said crisply. "Thy honor is dean!"

"My honor is in the dust!" Ram Singh said harshly. "But it shall be cleansed!"

Wentworth grinned, rested his hand for a moment on the brave Sikh's shoulder and left him, briefly recounting the story to Kirkpatrick. But phone calls failed to elicit any news of a knife killing.

"They probably took the body with them," Wentworth said. "I had hoped to have something definite with which to confront Don Carlos. Nita ...."

"I'm going with you, Dick," Nita said quietly. "I may be able to learn something from Doña Margherita. She used to like me."

Wentworth took in the firm set of her round chin, shrugged at Kirkpatrick's chuckle, but his hand on Nita's arm was gentle. He knew that her anxiety was all for him; that the privilege of sharing his danger was all she asked for from life — until that day when the *Spider* could write *finis* to his endless warfare with crime. He could not deny her now.

THE POLICE limousine carried them swiftly to the consulate, and Kirkpatrick signaled one of his watchers from the shadows. "There's considerable excitement and running around in there, sir," the man reported, "but they haven't called for police and they refused us entrance without a warrant. Sergeant Kilmer is waiting for orders from you."

Kirkpatrick nodded shortly. "Keep your post."

Wentworth listened silently, his eyes speculative, as he estimated time. As nearly as he could figure, there was a space of nearly an hour when there had been no watch over the consulate after the first visit of police, concerning Martinez's death. An hour in which... many things might have happened. The two men went swiftly up to the white door, Nita between them. A footman opened the door on a chain, peered out and recognized Wentworth.

"We'll have to speak to Don Carlos at once," Wentworth told him in Spanish.

The man jabbered at him a moment, closed the door. "He's gone to get the Doña Margherita," Wentworth said, frowning. "He said she had ordered no one admitted. That must mean that Don Carlos .... "

A rattle of the chain, the sound of the opening door interrupted, and Doña Margherita was hurrying along the foyer to meet them. Nita went forward, and the Spanish girl clasped both her hands tightly, turned to Wentworth.

"I am so glad you have come," she said swiftly. "I did not know what to do, whom to call. Señor Tavish—I have just reached him. He advised me to call on you at once, you and the commissioner of police .... "

Wentworth stepped forward swiftly, "This is Commissioner Kirkpatrick of the police," he said, feeling tension run along his arms. "What is the trouble? Is Don Carlos ... "

"How did you know?" Doña Margherita's face was very pale. She clung to Nita in seeming desperation.

"What has happened?" Wentworth repeated impatiently.

"Don Carlos .... "The girl shuddered. "There was a call from Señor Henry Lebland on business. My uncle .... Don Carlos .... "

Nita threw an arm around her. "It's all right now, dear," she said quietly. "Just tell them. They will know what to do."

Wentworth forced himself to be calm, to wait. His mind was casting swiftly about for an explanation. Perhaps, Carlos had known he was open to suspicion for his behavior—and had staged a disappearance. He eyed Margherita narrowly. If she were acting, it was a superb performance. Kirkpatrick was watching her closely, too.

"It is so horrible," she said in a strangled voice. "My uncle told me he must go to see Lebland on important business, that I could reach him there. He said I must admit no one while he was gone because we did not know why Señor Martinez had been . . . had been .... "

"Yes, yes, go on," Kirkpatrick cut in sharply.

Margherita drew in a deep breath. "My uncle went out to his car, which he had ordered around from the garage. When he stepped into it, I saw three men run from the shadows. They jumped in. I saw my uncle hit over the head, then one of those three men got behind a wheel and they drove away very fast, before I could send the men out to help him. And now . . . Oh, I am afraid they have killed him !"

Kirkpatrick asked curtly, "Your uncle's license number?"

Margherita gave it stumblingly, and Kirkpatrick hurried to the telephone with one of the footmen.

Wentworth still studied her. "I don't think you need fear that he has been killed, señiorita," he said softly. "Otherwise, they would not have bothered to kidnap him. Lebland exports munitions, doesn't he?"

"Oh, I do not know!" Margherita wailed. "I... do not know!"

Nita turned her toward the steps that led upward, threw Wentworth a significant backward glance. If the girl had any further information, Nita would get it. Wentworth strode after Kirkpatrick, heard him order Lebland brought to the consulate.

As he hung up, the phone rang shrilly. He turned. "Jackson. For you, Dick. He sounds . . . funny."

Wentworth seized the instrument, listened a moment. "Speak more clearly, Jackson. What's the matter? *Miles Scott!* Yes, yes... Stop laughing, Jackson, listen to me!" Wentworth's tones were edged, almost frantic. "Is there an odor of ozone in the room? An odor such as you get around dynamoes or after a lightning flash nearby? Jackson, listen! This is life and death! *Don't strike a match or fire a gun, no matter what happens!* You understand me? *No matter what happens!"*

Wentworth threw the phone into its cradle and whirled toward the door. His face was drawn and white.

"Miles Scott turned up at my house,"

he threw over his shoulder as he began to run. "And there is an odor of ozone in the house!"

Kirkpatrick gasped, "Great God, that means ...."

"It means the Master has turned loose his chemical against my home!" Wentworth snapped. "Jackson was already drunk with it. Unless we can get there in time, God knows what will happen!"

Wentworth sprang to the police car, with Kirkpatrick a half-stride behind, shouted an order at the driver. The siren began to whine.

"How much time have we?" Kirkpatrick demanded, his voice harsh.

"None at all," Wentworth shook his head. He was sitting far forward on the edge of the seat. "God help Jackson and the rest! We may already be too late!"

CHAPTER SIX
The Race Against Horror

TIME stood still while the mutter of the limousine's powerful engine deepened to a roar, while the siren's shriek wailed to a crescendo pitch that tortured the ears. Wentworth scarcely heard those things. He was straining forward on the seat as if his very will might urge the car to greater speed. Once his eyes flicked across the lighted dial of the speedometer and saw, with a sense of unbelief, that the needle hovered on eighty-two miles an hour.

"They're still safe, Dick!" Kirkpatrick shouted above the motor's fury and the rush of the wind. "If they weren't, we could see the fire glow. Shall I send a radio car ahead?"

"Couldn't get in," Wentworth replied tersely. "Jackson's too drunk on oxygen to open the gates. If we can get there before they tempt him to shoot and touch off the flames .... "

The car swung into Sutton Place, skidded half across its width before it wrenched into the straight-away again. Wentworth fingered a small silver whistle from his breast pocket. His eyes strained upward at the night sky. Not yet . . . But if a spark should fly, even after he entered the same room with Jackson, it would doom everyone within the house. His eyes grew cold.

"They'll wait until I'm inside," he said, with abrupt assurance. "And then ... touch-off. Kirk, stay with the car, please. You'll be able to shoot then if they open fire. Inside, it would mean death even to strike a match!"

Kirkpatrick's jaw set stubbornly. "It's undoubtedly a trap. It's madness for you to go inside the building. Madness!"

Wentworth didn't answer, and the limousine skidded into the sidestreet on which the gates of his home opened and he set the silver whistle to his lips.

"Don't slow down!" he called to the chauffeur. "Right up to the gates!"

He blew on the whistle, a piercing, peculiarly wavering note whose length he measured by the second hand of his watch. As he lowered the whistle, the car slued toward the gates and, with the smoothness of powerful mechanism, they slid swiftly open.

"Thought Jackson couldn't open the gates!" Kirkpatrick cried.

"Didn't," Wentworth snapped back. He shook the whistle. "Operated by sonics, too, in emergency. Stay where you can shoot."

The car's tires shrilled to a halt, and Wentworth was darting along the foyer, flinging into the elevator. Outside, guns began to blast! A harsh curse pushed from Wentworth's lips. Within seconds of his goal, but let one of those gas-besotted men above fire a gun in response! The elevator was one of the fastest ever made. Yet it *crawled* upward. He could hear shouting above him. Wentworth beat a fist into his palm. Seconds away— and he might be too late! He whipped his two automatics from his belt. He couldn't fire them, but once let him get in sight of Jackson and Miles Scott ....

The elevator door slid smoothly aside and Wentworth bounded through. His eyes flung desperately about the long room, half terrace, which ran toward the south gate. Jackson was crouched at a gun slit in the wall. He was shouting hoarsely. There was a revolver in his hand. Let him once pull that trigger ....

The air was thick with ozone. It made Wentworth's lungs pump wildly.

"Drop that gun, Jackson!" Wentworth cried. *"Drop it!"*

JACKSON seemed not to hear him. He was inching sideways, squinting along the barrel of the revolver and apparently following some moving figure, ready to fire the instant he was sure of his aim. Wentworth shouted again without effect. He whipped back his arm and flung one of his automatics. It was a desperate chance. He dared not throw at the head, lest the weight of the weapon crack Jackson's skull . . . and the hand was such a small target, pitifully small when lives dangled by that chance.

The dark-blue steel of the automatic seemed to hover in the air, suspended in the middle of the room, scarcely moving, though Wentworth had hurled it with the full sweep of his arm. Jackson was stationary now. It was plain he had his target. Tension rippled across his shoulders. He ground out a hoarse curse— and the automatic was just hanging there in the air, just hanging there ....

Wentworth was racing the length of the room, shouting. It was useless. If that automatic failed to strike in time— it it failed to hit Jackson's hand—he would be too late. Even with that certainty, Wentworth was sprinting at a pace even he had never equaled before. The thing was fantastic, impossible. He couldn't win this long race and fail now. He couldn't. The blasting of guns outside rose to a crescendo. At least one machine gun was hammering. But Kirkpatrick was safe enough behind those protecting walls. Safe enough—if the building didn't go up in flames!

The automatic struck—a miss! No, it had glanced from Jackson's elbow! His arm fell limply to his side; his gun plunged to the floor. Jackson's head twisted about. He groped for the revolver with his left hand and Wentworth took off in a long flying tackle. His shoulder caught Jackson's chest, drove him against the wall. The breath gasped from Jackson's lungs, his face darkened and he slumped, gasping, to the floor. His eyes were wide, and in them no sign of recognition. Wentworth fell to his knees, and struck

NITA VAN SLOAN

from that position, twice. Jackson slid sideways, unconscious, to the floor.

Wentworth could not pause. He sprang to his feet, spun about, eyes questing over the room. Jackson was alone, entirely alone. But Miles Scott and the old butler, Jenkyns? Wentworth sprang back along the room, heard a muffled thumping, a hoarse cry. It came from a small servingpantry off the entrance corridor, and he jerked at the door. Locked!

With swift understanding, he ran back to where Jackson lay, and hunted for the key. Jackson had done his best. He had locked up Jenkyns and Scott so that they could not possibly do any harm . . . but he had trusted himself too much.

Within minutes, Wentworth was back at the door. Miles Scott staggered out, leaned against the wall and began to laugh weakly. Jenkyns lay on the floor, breathing heavily. He tried to lift his head, with its cap of silvery hair, but the effort was too much for him. Wentworth darted past them to a bathroom, wet a towel and tied it over his nose and mouth, then hurried back. The air here was raw with oxygen. It stabbed the lungs at every breath. Without a word, he began to rip the clothing from Miles Scott's body. No doubt that the source of the gas was there. Presently, Scott was helping.

"Get into the bath," Wentworth gasped out. "Water will absorb oxygen."

He ran to the terrace with the clothing, hurled it far out. The wind caught the garments, whirled them like kites. One piece caught on the wall, held there for a moment flattened by wind pressure, then it was snatched over and beyond into the street. Flame flashed up to the heavens!

For a moment, a soft, hollow roaring filled the air. When that died, men were screaming, screaming in frantic agony! Wentworth flung doors and windows wide, went painfully to the elevator. He was laughing crazily when he staggered into open air, and Kirkpatrick ran toward him. It was minutes before he had control of himself and could lead Kirkpatrick inside.

JENKYNS was feebly on his feet, Jackson still unconscious and with a broken right arm from Wentworth's blow. Ram Singh was sleeping under an opiate. Wentworth sank down on a divan, feeling exhaustion in every nerve, but his brain refused rest. Swiftly, he recalled events of the last few hours. God! So many brave men had died in that short while, and the Master of the Flames... Wentworth strangled his anger, struggled for calm thought.

"The heaviest suspicion still attaches to Don Carlos," he told Kirkpatrick. "The kidnaping could have been faked, and I cannot make up my mind about Doña Margherita. She is intelligent. We will talk to Lebland when we get back to the consulate. Meantime, there is Humboldt Tavish. Really, there is very little against him, but I can't forget Beulah Loraine's fright when she looked at him. May have nothing to do with all this, of course."

Miles Scott had been fitted out with a uniform of Jackson's, already now under the care of Doctor Griggs, and he strode white-faced into the room.

"I don't know what to say, Mr. Wentworth," he began apologetically. "It's pretty plain that I brought that gas here, but I'll swear to you ...."

Wentworth smiled into the youth's frank face, liking him anew for his courage and the direct gaze of his blue eyes.

"Never mind," he interrupted Scott. "I know you were unaware the stuff was on your clothes. You can help a lot if you will try to find out how it got there. Tell me what happened."

Scott's words poured out swiftly. He had taken Beulah home, gone to his own rooms to bed, then worrying, had arisen, dressed and returned to the girl's apartment. When he arrived, men were putting Ram Singh into an ambulance and it had taken Scott a long while to learn what had happened to the Sikh. He had guessed Beulah's fate and, in desperation, come to ask Wentworth's help.

"If anyone can help me, sir," he finished, "it's you. Or if we could get in touch with the *Spider* . . . Oh, I know you ought to throw me out on my ear for bringing that gas here, but I hope ...."

"I'll do what I can," Wentworth told him quietly, "but to find Beulah, we'll have to find the man behind these fire outrages! The Master! You can help. That gas was in your clothing. Find out how it got there. And one other thing." His eyes held keenly on Scott's face. "Beulah was afraid of Humboldt Tavish, and now she has been kidnaped. Do you know why ... she was afraid?"

Scott's face registered only amazement. "Tavish? You mean the fat man at the consulate? Was she afraid?"

Wentworth frowned, "I think that when we know why she was afraid," he said slowly, "we'll know why Beulah was kidnaped. Perhaps the answers to many other things."

He sent Scott off then to learn how the Master had tricked them with the gas, and he and Kirkpatrick sped back to the consulate. Kirkpatrick was frowning.

"This Humboldt Tavish," he said slowly. "There's really not enough against him to warrant putting him over the hurdles. Do you think he's involved deeply?"

"I doubt," Wentworth answered him softly, "that even the *Spider* would consider that there was sufficient reason for action."

Kirkpatrick brushed his spiked mustaches with a knuckle of his right hand. "I'm glad to hear it," he said dryly.

HENRY LEBLAND rose wordlessly at their entrance into the reception room of the consulate. He was a thin-faced man, sardonic of mien, with an irritating trick of lifting his eyebrows superciliously. His hair was dark, reddish, smooth.

"I really don't mind doing anything I can to help enforce the law," he said, and there was a sneer in his voice, "but I left a number of guests at home and you've kept me waiting precisely one hour and five minutes."

Wentworth stared. Commissioner Kirkpatrick bowed, his face expressionless. "You telephoned Don Carlos earlier this evening?"

"You know damned well I did," Lebland said curtly.

A dark flush began to mount Kirkpatrick's cheeks, but his tone remained flat,

"What about?"

"Business!"

Kirkpatrick said dryly, "So I inferred."

The men's eyes met directly, and there was anger in both. Wentworth surveyed the man openly. Before an embargo had been placed on arms, he had been shipping huge quantities to the Loyalists in Spain and there was small reason to think that he had stopped the commerce subsequently, despite the close watch of the United States government men. But it was hard to understand how he would profit from kidnaping the representative of the Loyalists, Don Carlos.

It was plain that Kirkpatrick was keeping his voice under control only by great effort. "Let's understand each other, Lebland," he said, crisply. "Don Carlos has been kidnaped. The phone call that put him on the spot was yours. Unless you make prompt and satisfactory explanations, I'll have you summoned before the grand jury and forced to talk under oath. You can refuse to talk only on these grounds—that it might incriminate yourself. Do you wish to claim exemption?"

Lebland lifted his eyebrows and smiled slightly. "I might," he said quietly.

"Do you know, Kirkpatrick," Wentworth interjected, "whether Doña Margherita has put through the call to Washington yet? I have an idea the Federal Bureau of Investigation might like to ask some questions, too."

Lebland swung toward him slowly and for all the sardonic amusement on his face, there was a stab of anger in his eyes.

"Call the G-men and be damned to you," he said shortly. He swung back to

Kirkpatrick. "Why do you petty politicians always have to do things in such a high-handed way? If you had come to me decently instead of hauling me half across the city this way, taking me away from my guests, I might be inclined to be decent, too. I'm not a criminal. And I decline to be treated like one!"

Kirkpatrick dropped his eyes to hide a flicker of amusement. "I'm sorry," he said quietly, "but this is a grave matter. Don Carlos' disappearance seems to be involved in a case in which more than twenty men have been killed in the last several hours. I have been a bit... rushed."

"Twenty men killed!" Lebland cried. "Why, what... I'm sorry, Commissioner. What did you want to know?"

After that, the story came out smoothly enough. Don Carlos had been coöperating with him in extensive shipments to Spain and another was going out in a few days. Don Carlos was handling the payments; money had failed to come through, and he was due to come to Lebland's home. When he failed to show, Lebland had phoned.

"I can give you details, Commissioner," Lebland finished, "if you wish. Frankly, I'd rather not give them. But I can assure you I have every reason for not wanting Don Carlos to disappear at this particular time. If you wish to go into the matter further, I'll have to consult with my attorneys and with my more or less silent partner."

Wentworth was lighting a cigarette and he did not lift his eyes from the operation. "Might I ask, Mr. Lebland," he said quietly, "if your partner's name is Humboldt Tavish?"

His eyes brushed over Lebland as he pronounced the name, and he saw Lebland's face go blank of all expression.

Lebland said stiffly, "I am not at liberty to say."

When he had gone, Kirkpatrick said, very deliberately, "I think it's time we had a talk with Tavish. Dick, you're positively uncanny."

Wentworth smiled slightly, though there were somber depths in his eyes. "If you'll take a bit of uncanny advice, Kirk," he said, "let's not talk to Tavish until tomorrow. We'll do it at his office. Meantime, set men to watch him—men who are not too smart."

Kirkpatrick frowned. "Damn it, Dick," he said, "this is no time for riddles."

Wentworth shook his head. "No riddle. The idea is to let Tavish know that he's watched. Smart men wouldn't be spotted. A worried antagonist sometimes makes blunders."

A slow smile moved Kirkpatrick's firm lips. "I know just the men for the job."

Nita van Sloan remained at the consulate at the insistence of Doña Margherita, and Kirkpatrick put a police guard over the building. Nevertheless, Wentworth was not satisfied. Danger at the consulate was not over, he felt confident; though, as he pointed out to Kirkpatrick, it was entirely possible that Don Carlos had arranged for his own kidnaping.

EVEN when they left the consulate, there were hours of work before Wentworth could get a little needed sleep at his home. Chemists were set to work in an effort to arrive at the basis for the fires, a number of the scarlet garments of the Flame Men were being analyzed and attempts made to trace them. The immigration department was called upon to identify the dead, if possible, and make a thorough check of all arrivals from Spain during the last year. Other men were set to work to trace the armored cars which the looters had used, to find Beulah and Don Carlos. In this latter phase also, the government was coöperating.

Wentworth approved these routine inquiries, but doubted that, even if any succeeded, it would point to the Master himself. Finding a subordinate would help not at all. Those who failed the Master died too horribly for any of his men to be encouraged to talk! The only chance for the forces of the law was to discover a way to combat the fire and hope doggedly for a break . . . A bitter smile touched Wentworth's chiseled lips. While they hoped, the Master would strike again and again! His ruthless weapon could destroy entire cities of people, could wreck a nation!

Damnable to be so helpless, but, for the present, the police were doing more than the *Spider* could accomplish single-handed. Suspicion did not yet attach to any one man sufficiently to permit the *Spider* to strike. If he might absolutely verify a single point, he could set to work. But those who had clues were removed before he could even reach them —the two assassins, Beulah Loraine, Don Carlos. If Doña Margherita knew any-

thing, Nita would learn it much more quickly than he. Lebland had behaved suspiciously, but it was apparent his concern was over his smuggling arms past the American embargo to aid the Spanish. Humboldt Tavish alone remained.

It was close to three o'clock the next afternoon when Wentworth drove with Kirkpatrick to Tavish's elaborate office. It was one of those suites, as luxurious as a sultan's bower, which seemed more suited to amorous dalliance than to business. The reception clerk spoke in hushed cathedral tones. She was sorry, but Mr. Tavish was holding a meeting of the board of directors. She would, if they insisted, send in their names.

Kirkpatrick said, with a slight smile, "I do insist." He turned to Wentworth as the girl tiptoed out. "There's too much front here. It looks phony."

Wentworth agreed with a curt nod, his mind skimming again over the information he had garnered about Tavish. *Who's Who* knew him statistically and gave a list of directorates, the chief of which was his chairmanship of the board of the Investment Holding Company. Newspapers and police had been able to add little more. He was not married, but was reported engaged to Doña Margherita.

Disapproval had gone from the reception girl's face when she returned. "I'm to show you into Mr. Tavish's private office," she whispered. "He'll recess the board in a few moments and join you!"

THE room in which the board of directors met was more austere than the rest of the suite, but each item of its furnishings was extremely rich. The long table was of solid San Domingo mahogany and the tapestry of the upholstered chairs rare old *petit point*. It may have been for this reason that smoking was prohibited during sessions of the board, though certain shrewd members believed this was a device of Humboldt Tavish, who did not smoke, to shorten the meetings and so give himself more rein. Color was lent to that theory by the fact that, during the recesses, smoking was allowed. It is strange what things men will concede when they want a smoke badly enough...

It is a fact that the directors dreaded the meetings, but on this particular day there was a full attendance since an important matter was scheduled: an investment which, while hazardous, could triple the money staked if it was brought off. Discussion was far more animated than over any previous issue in months. Laughter boomed in the room—laughter that at times sounded cracked, even a bit silly. In fact, they all behaved as if they were a little... *drunk*. Humboldt Tavish had just told them so with some acerbity when he received the message from Commissioner Kirkpatrick. Tavish rose to his feet, his moon face flushed.

"Gentlemen!" he cried sharply, "are you ready to vote this issue?"

The grey-haired man on his right giggled. "0, beg your pardon, Tavish," he giggled again. "But your face looks precisely like an out-size Edam cheese!"

For a moment deep silence fell upon the directors' room, then a storm of laughter burst. Tavish slammed down the gavel. He heaved his chair aside and strode from the room. The grey-haired man fumbled for a cigarette.

"I assume," he said with mock gravity, "that we are now in recess, gentlemen." He giggled again, drunkenly, as he put the cigarette to his lips. He held his lighter gravely before his face and fingered the flame mechanism ....

IN HUMBOLDT TAVISH'S private office, Wentworth listened, frowning, to the faint sound of merriment that reached him through the thick walls. "A strange board meeting," he murmured to Kirkpatrick.

The commissioner was frowning, too, and the laughter blurted on a louder note, shut off as an almost concealed door opened to admit Tavish.

"Imbeciles!" he cried violently. "They act as if they were all drunk . . . I beg your pardon, gentlemen, but—"

Wentworth caught him by the arm and felt fear race coldly up his spine. "As if they were drunk!" he cried harshly. "Does the air smell very fresh like ... like *ozone!*"

Tavish stared at him, his small blue eyes stretching wide. He looked extraordinarily like a bald, startled baby. "Why, now that you mention it ...."

Wentworth sprang toward the door and whipped it open. "Don't strike a match!" he shouted. "If you value your lives, don't ...."

Strong hands caught Wentworth by the shoulders and whipped him back. He heard Kirkpatrick's voice grinding out oaths and, reeling, saw his friend jam the door shut with his shoulder. The clap of its closing raised an overwhelming echo, a deep, booming explosion that seemed to bend the door against its hinges. Flame sheeted out about its edges. Kirkpatrick shrank from the heat, covering his face. Tavish's cry was that of a man torn on the rack. And beyond the door, the roaring of flames mingled with screams.

All these things happened while Wentworth fought for balance from Kirkpatrick's throw. He saw Tavish leap for the telephone, but Kirkpatrick was ahead of him. Wentworth heard his crisp voice bark out, "Police headquarters!

Fast!"

Wentworth ran toward the outer door, raced through the reception office and into the public hall. Within seconds, he had wrenched a coiled fire hose from its rack, spun the water valve and was charging back. Flames were eating throughh the door, and the hose's stream punched out charred wood, raked through into the area beyond. But, quick as he had been, the screams within already were stilled.

Kirkpatrick's crisp voice was rolling out orders to close every exit of the building, to let no one out until there had been a personal examination of each. Grimly, Wentworth kept playing the hose into the directors' room, inching closer to the door.

The crash of a gun cut off Kirkpatrick's voice in mid-word. Wentworth spun about, reaching for his automatic.

"Freeze like that, both of you gentlemen," a voice ordered coldly. "Tavish, you human balloon, stand still!"

The voice came from beyond the open outer door of the office and, through the narrow opening, jutted the muzzle of a sub-machine gun. Incredulously, Wentworth saw that from that source came a flickering, lurid-light as if there, too, the flames were at work. As he stared, the door pushed wider and, with a long stride, one of the Flaming Horde entered the office. His suit was scarlet and all about his body spurted loops and tongues of flame!

Even though Wentworth knew now the secret of those scarlet garments, gleaned from those of the Flame Men he had slain, the effect was terrifying. The suits were asbestos basically, blended with some other strange substances; the flames came from a score of jets fed under pressure from an alcohol tank so that they had no actual point of contact with the suit itself. Wentworth told himself these things deliberately as, twisted awkwardly about, he gazed at the man in the doorway. And yet it was hard to believe *that* figure was human. Like some demon out of deepest hell, he strode into the room and, above him, the doorway charred and burst into flame!

"It is well," came the man's mocking voice, "that you obey the words of . . . the Master!"

The machine gun's muzzle swung idly, and Tavish gasped and dropped into a chair as if he were in truth a human balloon, punctured. Kirkpatrick stood rigid with anger, and Wentworth saw that the single shot had smashed the telephone to bits. His mind was working in flashes. If this really were the Master, the man should never escape alive from this room! But that sub-machine gun . . .

SWIFTLY, Wentworth conned the situation. Kirkpatrick stood behind the desk, pinned there helplessly by the gun. Tavish was out of the picture, and Wentworth, his back three-quarters turned toward the Master, both bands on the hose which still played into the directors' room, was in the worst possible position to strike.

The hose was his obvious weapon, but its roaring pressure made it impossible to aim quickly. The entire weight of his body was necessary to handle it and long before he could swing it against the Master, the machine gun would cut him in half. His own automatic would be swifter, but the released hose would give advance warning of any move he made. He had to act quickly! The Master would not delay long. Already, the fumes and heat were strangling Wentworth. He coughed rackingly and heard the Master laugh. And, suddenly, Wentworth saw the way!

"Señores," said the Master, "I shall grant you one minute for prayers!"

Wentworth swore savagely at him. He coughed, and the hose wavered in his hands. Its powerful stream missed the hole in the door through which it had been pouring, struck the wood and the recoil seemed to tear it from Wentworth's hands. It writhed like a live thing, struck his side and knocked him to the floor.

Even through the roar of the gushing water, Wentworth could hear the Master's high, mocking laughter. Wentworth's lips set savagely. As he fell, his hands were busy. In an instant, they had flashed to his holsters. A quick bunching of his legs beneath him, a spring and he was half behind the desk. His automatic roared!

No time for a head shot. He had to paralyze the Master instantly with his lead before the machine gun could stammer out its stream of death. Both automatics spoke together and their bullets converged on the pit of the Master's stomach—a *solar plexus* punch of lead!

Doubled over, the Master was hurled backward through the doorway! His machine gun dropped to the floor—and Wentworth was fighting for his life! Through that doorway, lead screamed from a half dozen guns. A splinter of wood tore from the desk within an inch of Wentworth's head. Kirkpatrick crouched behind the desk, his long-barreled revolver speaking.

Wentworth also dodged behind its protection, straining his eyes for a target. The smoke was dense in the office now. It stung his eyes, burned in his lungs. He threw a sidewise glance at Tavish and saw that the man had rolled from his chair—and off to one side, was fighting with the hose. He had gripped it several feet back from the nozzle and the end of it writhed like a serpent, the stream striking the ceiling, then the floor . . . but Tavish was winning his fight.

Wentworth shouted encouragement and began to hammer blind lead through the doorway. Let Tavish once get that hose under control, and they could pound the gunmen outside into submission without needing to see them. Dimly, through the smoke, he tried to locate the Master's body. Not much chance of a man surviving the double dynamite of two .45 caliber bullets through his stomach and diaphragm, but it was barely possible the Master wore bullet-proof armor under that scarlet garb . . . and the *Spider* did not intend that the Master should escape!

Through the haze, he glimpsed a scarlet-clad figure prostrate upon the floor and, lips thinned back from his teeth, he deliberately pumped five more bullets into throat and head. Grim? Merciless? Yes, all of that, but the Master had killed a score of brave men. In this next room lay the charred bodies of a dozen more. When he faced such a criminal, the *Spider* was the avenging arm of destiny itself!

Tavish had the hose near its nozzle now, and the powerful stream was beating through the door. Strangled curses came from beyond. Wentworth thrust fresh clips into his automatic, reached Tavish's side in a bound and backed that water barrage with his unerring bullets. Kirkpatrick sprang to the doorway. Side by side, they swept the room beyond clean of enemies. Three scarlet-clad bodies were on the floor. Wentworth bounded across to the outer door, but the hall was empty . . ..

Moments later, police came storming up stairways and elevators, Sergeant Reams with them.

"All exits closed, Commissioner," he reported curtly. "They won't get away!"

Both automatics spoke together and their bullets converged on the Master.

KIRKPATRICK turned back with Wentworth to the three Flame Men on the floor of the office. With efficient hands, Wentworth stripped off the uniforms. The first man was the one into whom he had thrown an entire clip of bullets. He bore only head wounds! Wentworth hurried to the other dead. Not one of them bore the mark of the two bullets Wentworth had thrown into the *solar plexus* of the Master!

"He got away!" Wentworth swore. "He must have worn armor!"

"He didn't walk for a while after those two bullets punched him, even if he did wear armor," Kirkpatrick said grimly. "We'll get him!"

They swung to go, and Wentworth's eyes fell on Tavish. The man was utterly broken. He slumped in a chair, his moon face wet with tears. Wentworth crossed and put a hand gently on his shoulder.

"It's horrible, I know," he said kindly, "but you have the satisfaction of knowing that if you hadn't handled the hose, we couldn't have made it."

Tavish's face lifted heavily, "My friends," he said thickly. "All my friends... burned to death."

Kirkpatrick said, flatly, "They'll be avenged!"

He strode rapidly from the office, and Wentworth followed to the elevators. The first-floor corridor was packed with police and a group of civilians was filing, one by one, past a magazine and cigar booth which had been hurriedly commandeered as a desk. Their identities were being checked. Kirkpatrick went directly to the booth.

"Has anyone been released at all?" he demanded curtly.

The sergeant scrambled to his feet. "No one, Commissioner," he said crisply, "except two injured porters the firemen carried to an ambulance."

Wentworth swore and darted toward the exit. As he burst into the street, an ambulance spun away around the corner, siren wailing, and bored through the traffic. On the pavement, an interne lay unconscious, his head bleeding.

"Stop that ambulance!" Wentworth shouted. "Stop it if you have to shoot!"

Kirkpatrick reached his side an instant later and echoed the order, and policemen darted toward their cars. Kirkpatrick's own machine was pinned to the curb by a half dozen others and it was long seconds before it could be cleared.

WENTWORTH'S jaw was locked. He reloaded his automatics with steady hands. It was easy to follow the wake of screaming sirens and, one after another, the racing radio coupes fell behind the powerful limousine of the commissioner.

The route lay straight north along Broadway, swung westward to Church as they left the financial district behind. Traffic skittered aside and the speedometer of the limousine showed sixty, seventy, seventy-five... The ambulance was in sight now, its siren shrieking like a beast in pain. As the limousine began to close the gap, a gun hammered from the rear window of the hospital car.

Wentworth laughed softly and crawled through into the seat beside the chauffeur, leaned out around the edge of the windshield. Then he waited as the limousine lunged across cobbles, streaked through the parted traffic of Canal Street and straightened out two blocks behind the ambulance. The range was still long for the automatics.

"Wide open!" Wentworth snapped at the chauffeur.

Under him, the limousine surged and

the roar of the motor took on a deeper note. A block behind the ambulance now, Wentworth began to shoot. They were dangerously close now to the point at which the Sixth Avenue elevated turned into the broad street ahead. The limousine closed the gap with violent speed. A shot from the ambulance made a frosted spot as big as an orange on the bulletproof windshield. Another whanged on the hood and gouged a silvery furrow.

Wentworth was using his second automatic, and his first shot brought a scream that the wind whipped back to their ears. He fired again, and the ambulance, like a living, wounded thing, skittered sideways, brushed an elevated pillar, bounced and caught a second pillar broadside. The wreck bounded back twenty feet, teetered on two wheels. The limousine's brakes were locked, its tires screaming.

"Brace yourself!" Wentworth shouted. He put his shoulder against the windshield and an instant later, the police machine slammed into the wreck, and sent it in a slow, end-over-end turn back toward the pillar. When it struck this time, it remained there.

Wentworth reeled a little as he sprang to the pavement, but he steadied at once as he strode toward the wreck, gun in hand.

For the first time, he was conscious of a scream. It bored piercingly up into the burning sunlight, stopped for the space of a quick breath, started again. It kept up. There was no other evidence of life. The ambulance was a mass of junk, scarcely identifiable as an automobile. Kirkpatrick's crisp stride kept pace with Wentworth's, as he moved on. The scream kept on... *scream,* breath, *scream* ....

Sirens wailed up, died as other police cars converged on the spot. Men in blue began to turn traffic aside, others climbed over the wreck. There were three men inside—the *remnants* of three men. One wore the uniform of a building porter, the other two those of firemen. His face set in a rigid mold, Wentworth stood by while those bodies were examined and at the end, he turned with a violent curse.

"Not one of them is the Master!" he said bitterly. "He would have either bullet wounds in the abdomen or else a deep bruise if he wore armor. The Master has escaped!"

CHAPTER SEVEN
Disaster!

A LAZY haze of snow was beginning to fall as Wentworth and Kirkpatrick raced back to the financial district in a prowl car commandeered after the limousine was wrecked. Almost before the car jerked to a halt at the office building, Kirkpatrick was shouting orders to throw a cordon around the entire district and trap the Master. A close check on hospitals and doctors also was ordered.

The check on persons in the building was going forward slowly, though it was reasonably certain that all of the criminals, whom the swift guns of Wentworth and Kirkpatrick had not slain already, had gone in the ambulance. Wentworth smiled wryly, as he entered an elevator with Kirkpatrick.

"Perhaps if we keep on killing a few of them every day," he said, "we'll reach the Master eventually."

Kirkpatrick knuckled his mustache. "We're getting nowhere, Dick—nowhere," he said. "Surely, you can't suspect Tavish any longer? He helped us fight the Flame Men!"

Wentworth shrugged, "He's Lebland's partner in the munitions venture, but except for the accident of our arrival, he would have been killed with the other directors. The Master, himself, apparently came there to make sure Tavish died."

Kirkpatrick said grimly, "I still want to ask Tavish some questions."

The fire had been entirely extinguished when they returned to Tavish's offices. Flames and water had made a mess of the lavish suite. The entire directors' room was badly charred and the long table itself reduced to ashes!

"It looks," Wentworth pointed out, "as if the table had been the source of flame. Have the chemists made any progress in identifying the flame chemical?"

Kirkpatrick shook his head, pushed on to the outer office, where Humboldt Tavish, still pale and shaken, was directing the staff in an attempt to straighten out the firm's records. At Kirkpatrick's request, he dismissed his workers.

"I'll be frank with you," Kirkpatrick said curtly. "We came here because we suspected you of having a hand in Don Carlos' disappearance. You will admit that you're Lebland's partner in munition smuggling, I think."

Tavish lifted his fat shoulders in a shrug. "That was the question the board was discussing at the time the fire started. I think they would have voted to finance Lebland all right, but now . . . You can't be serious about Don Carlos?"

"He was kidnaped when he went out in answer to a call from Lebland," Kirkpatrick told him shortly. "It could be possible that you had Lebland call him."

"But, good God!" Tavish struggled to his feet. "Don Carlos is the uncle of the woman I love! Surely, you don't think... Damn it, it's preposterous!"

"Tavish," Wentworth cut in softly, "why was it that police were called so late after the attack on Martinez and myself?

You were at the consulate." He was watching Tavish's face closely, but it revealed only blank surprise, a rising indignation.

"Didn't you know that?" Tavish asked, his voice amazed. "Don Carlos sent a man to the phone and someone hit him over the head. We found him much later. The poor fellow didn't see who did it. As soon as we learned about it, I called you."

Wentworth swore under his breath, and Kirkpatrick listened, narrow-eyed. "Martinez was all right when you got there, Tavish?" he asked harshly.

Tavish sank into his chair again. "I thought he had been drinking a bit too much. He became quite boisterous. I seem to remember Don Carlos..." His small mouth snapped shut.

"You'll finish that sentence," Kirkpatrick ordered shortly. "If Don Carlos is guilty, no one can protect him."

"It wasn't anything," Tavish said hurriedly. "Just that Don Carlos told Martinez that since he couldn't control himself in the presence of guests, he'd better leave. 'Take a walk and sober up', was his exact phrase, I believe."

Wentworth's eyes met Kirkpatrick's, and the commissioner nodded. "I think we know enough," he said curtly. He swung striding toward the door, and Tavish's deep voice rolled after him.

"You're wrong, dead wrong," he called doggedly. "Don Carlos isn't guilty of anything, but ...."

KIRKPATRICK didn't speak to Wentworth while the elevator dropped to the main floor. As the door opened, a man wrenched free from a uniformed policeman and darted toward them. It was Miles Scott. His square face was flushed with excitement. "I've had the devil of a time getting to you," he cried. "I think I've got a clue as to how they use this fire chemical!"

Scott's story came out swiftly. When he had returned home, the apartment building in which he lived was in flames! It took him hours to locate the superintendent and get him to talk.

"The only person who entered my apartment that night was a man who said he was from the exterminator. It wasn't his regular time to come!" Scott was almost shouting words. "And he went over the entire apartment building... *at night!*"

"That sounds like it!" Wentworth cried. Kirkpatrick's jaw set angrily. "Of all fool things! Why did the superintendent allow it?"

Scott laughed sharply. "That's exactly it! The man had some story about a new system—using it at night because that was when insects came out of hiding. And he insisted on *spraying my closet and clothes!*"

"*A* spray!" Wentworth exclaimed triumphantly. "Scott, this is valuable, I think the attack on me was an afterthought. After you entered my place, they decided on an attempt to trap me. Kirk, I think I've hit on some new lines of inquiry. Shall we go to your office?"

Kirkpatrick's frosty eyes flicked to him briefly. "God knows I'd be glad of anything that might shed light on this business and put an end to the slaughter. Come along, Scott."

WENTWORTH began to outline his ideas as soon as the detective cruiser Kirkpatrick took over was under way. "At first," he said, "I thought these fires were merely a criminal weapon to help in looting, but the murder of that board of directors doesn't fit into that theory. I'd like to check all the holdings of Tav ish's

company; watch the heirs of the board and see who acquires the directors' stock. It would have to be done inconspicuously."

"Still suspecting Tavish?" Kirkpatrick demanded impatiently.

Wentworth shrugged. "I'm not inclined to. Another thing, we can try to trace that exterminator, so called. And I imagine the Master will have to recruit some domestic criminals for his work soon. Almost every man we've traced has been Spanish and we've killed quite a few. He'll need more. Stool pigeons might give you a lead there."

Routine, all of it routine—and slow! Day by day, the terror of the Flame Men would increase... The radio whine pulled his attention to sharp focus.

"Number One," the announcer called. "Report for Number One. Pittsburgh reports three steel mills razed by fires of suspicious origin. The mills are ...."

Kirkpatrick explained briefly that he had requested that reports on all large fires, wherever they occurred, be made to him immediately, but Wentworth was concentrating on the names of the mills....

"This is in line with what I was urging," he said excitedly. "Destruction of steel mills can't have any connection with looting! The thing has a financial background, and . . . By the heavens, Kirk, doesn't the Fairlands family control one of those banks that was looted yesterday?" Kirkpatrick frowned, "I think so."

"They own those steel mills also!" Wentworth cried. "Maybe this is the break we've been looking for! Check on the other holdings of that family! Get in touch with them to learn if they have any financial enemies who might strike this way! It seems to me they're interested in a steamship line and own a large block of some railroad. Keep a close check on the trading in Wall Street in all shares the

DON CARLOS   LEBLAND   TAVISH

Fairlands holdings!"

Kirkpatrick was sitting bolt upright now. "You may have something there, Dick." He called sharply to the driver. "Faster, there, man! Work that siren!"

The radio whined again, "Number One! I have an important phone call. Please call headquarters at once."

"What the devil can that be?" Kirkpatrick's voice was edged.

He shifted anxiously on the seat. This car was not equipped with two-way radio, as was his private machine. He shouted at the driver again, but it was ten minutes before the sedan halted at headquarters, two more before he could reach his office. He called an order at his secretary to get the phone call and, as he reached his desk, the signal buzzed. He snapped up the receiver. Wentworth stood watching quietly. Miles Scott, beside him, was taut with excitement.

"Nita!" Kirkpatrlck exclaimed, his eyes going to Wentworth. "Yes . . . Give me that number again... Yes, at once. Thanks, Nita. Dick's here, if ...." He hung up.

"She disconnected," he told Wentworth. "She says that Doña Margherita received a note or letter by messenger. She burned the message and immediately called this phone number. Nita couldn't understand what was said because the girl spoke some unfamiliar dialect of Spanish, but she's almost sure it was Don Carlos at the other end of the wire!"

"Good for Nita!" Wentworth exclaimed. "Scott, this may give us a lead to Beutah!"

Kirkpatrick rang for his secretary and tossed at him the slip of paper with the phone number.

"Find the address of that number at

DOÑA MARGHERITA   BEULAH LORAINE   MILES SCOTT

once." His voice crackled with energy. "Tell Sergeant Reams I'll need a raiding-squad of a dozen men at once!"

ACROSS the room, the bell of a tele-type machine, connected with all boroughs of the city, began to jangle excitedly. Wentworth reached it in a stride. Kirkpatrick peered over his shoulder and a curse rasped fiercely in his throat.

"A three-alarm fire at Union Central station!" he cried. "Reams will have to handle that phone call tip alone."

Wentworth stood motionless as Kirkpatrick strode toward the door. "Do you mind?" he asked slowly. "I'll go with Reams and join you later at the fire. I have an idea this phone call is important!"

Kirkpatrick's secretary came hurriedly in. "Here's that address, Commiss-ioner," he said swiftly. "It's a public phone in a beer saloon called 'Frank's Place'. It's on the Bowery, near Chatham Square!"

Wentworth swore softly, and Kirkpatrick curtly canceled the orders for a squad of raiders. "Might have guessed something like that! A public phone!"

Wentworth shrugged. "I'll go with you after all, Kirk." They were in the car together before they realized Miles Scott was not with them. There was no time to delay and the car rolled without him. The autumn dusk was settling fast. A thickening pattern of snow flakes whipped toward them, turned redly ominous by the police car's tinted headlights.

Wentworth said quietly, "The National Trunk railway has its freight terminal at Union Central station. The Fairlands practically own the National

Trunk."

Kirkpatrick whipped about toward him, "I'll order that check-up as soon as I get back to headquarters."

Wentworth said shortly, "With your permission, I'll phone that order to head-quarters as soon as we stop. Damn it, Kirk, every hour is valuable! How long can this sort of thing keep up before virtual anarchy begins? You know your men are too busy to watch any criminals except the men of the Master! And don't think the underworld won't understand and take advantage of it! You're going to have a full-sized crime wave—hell, a tidal wave!—unless we check the Master and do it soon!"

Kirkpatrick's eyes saw the burning northward. Already the glow of fire was smearing bloodily across the evening sky.

"From what Scott found out," Kirkpatrick clipped out, "the chemical is a liquid. It could be sprayed down-wind on the station from a high building and pass unseen in this snowfall."

"Right!" Wentworth agreed. "The Keystone Spire is northeast—upwind—of the Union Central! If they waited for the snow, they can't have begun this long ago. Flame Men may still be there."

Kirkpatrick's voice rang harshly, "Driver, stop at that corner cigarstore. Dick, I'll lock that building up so tight a flea can't get out! And I'll personally knock the head off any man who lets any-one slip through!"

Wentworth followed him into the store and heard the orders. "Now, Kirk," he said quickly, "tell them I'll give some further instructions. I want to start that check-up on the Fairlands. I'll also order a guard for the steamship-line piers and have police warned in other cities where there are railway or ship properties."

KIRKPATRICK threw the requisite authorization into the telephone and went striding back to the sedan. There was a tight frown on his forehead. Damn it, Dick Wentworth was right! Criminal anarchy did threaten! This was the second day of the reign of the fire terror and al-ready reports of crimes had literally dou-bled. Let this horror keep up for a few more days, for a week . ..

Kirkpatrick arrived at the Keystone Spire simultaneously with the second radio patrol car sent out on his orders.

The men sprang to the doors of the main entrance and began locking them. Kirkpatrick strode to a side entrance and turned people back.

"The entire building is surrounded by the police," he said harshly. "There has been a big robbery and every man will have to account for himself before we can let anyone go. I'm sorry."

Within two minutes, a squad car rolled to the door, and there were enough men to stop all exits. Kirkpatrick picked up a sergeant and two other uniformed men and entered an elevator. The most likely place for the spray work would be high up.

"Top floor!" he snapped at the opera-tor of the elevator. "No stops. You men, get your guns in your hands. Don't hesi-tate to shoot anyone who fails to stop when challenged."

The police officers drew their guns silently and the sergeant crowded in front of Kirkpatrick. "Excuse me, Commis-sioner, but there may be danger ...."

For a moment, Kirkpatrick's expres-sion softened. Such samples of the loyal-ty of his men were the rule rather than the exception.

"I'm not sure what we're running into," he said. "I think the chemical which caused the fire was sprayed out of this building. You can tell the presence of the chemical by a freshness in the air. Ozone, if you're familiar with it. If you should smell that, don't shoot under any provocation. It would start a holocaust!"

The sergeant sniffed energetically. "It seems to me, Commissioner, that the air smells *fresh* right now," he said.

Kirkpatrick stared at him with the beginning of a smile around his straight lips, then swiftly frowned. The man was right. There was a definitely fresher odor here! The operator whipped open the door, as the car came to a halt at the top floor and Kirkpatrick stepped out. The odor was no stronger. Probably from the burning station, Kirkpatrick decided. He singled out a man.

"Stand guard here," he said curtly. "Let no one leave this floor. I don't think there's any danger in shooting unless the odor gets much stronger than it is now."

A tension braced Kirkpatrick's body, and he felt exhilaration creep through him. This odor was pretty definite proof that he had guessed right. They might trap some of the Master's men here, might even find some of the chemical!

"Shoot to cripple, not to kill," he said briskly. "I'd like to have a chance to question one of those men!"

The sergeant laughed, "I'd like to help you, sir!"

Swiftly, they made a canvass of the offices on the floor. Most were occupied, but there was no trace of spray mechanism or tanks which might contain the chemical. As Kirkpatrick strode toward the steps to the roof, he glanced at an elevator boy, who leaned against the open door of his cage, waiting for the signal to descend. There was a wide grin on his face. He giggled, and Kirkpatrick's eyes went back to him sharply.

"What's the matter with you?"

"Not a thing," the boy protested. "I feel swell!" He giggled again and, getting his signal from the starter below, slammed the door. Kirkpatrick stared at the closed door a long moment, then shrugged.

"Now the roof," he ordered. His stride lengthened. He sucked air deeply into his lungs. "I think we're going to be lucky, Sergeant," he said crisply.

The sergeant laughed. "Sure, Commissioner," he said. "Sure."

He laughed again, and Kirkpatrick felt his own mouth corners stir. The wind on the roof was brisk. It flung snow into Kirkpatrick's face. He bowed his head into it, stood peering alertly about. The towering flames of the burning terminal threw a flickering glare. It took only a few moments to find that the roof was bare of other human life. There were no other foot prints in the snow. Impatiently, Kirkpatrick led the way back to the top floor. Two girls were talking to the police guard. There was a wide grin on the man's face. The girls swayed on their feet. The patrolman looked up into the commissioner's face.

"They think it's going to snow all night," the man said rapidly, and giggled.

KIRKPATRICK stared at him and felt tension crawl along his muscles. He seized the man by the arms, peered into his face, whirled toward the two girls. They watched him with bright eyes, laughing, laughing ....

Kirkpatrick felt the blood drain from his face. Good God, was the ozone increasing? He sniffed and could not tell. He recalled with a sickening sense of cold in his stomach that the olfactory nerves quickly became blunted to a continuous odor. He whirled toward the sergeant.

"Do you notice that ozone odor more

strongly?" he demanded.

An elevator door slammed open, and Wentworth sprang out into the hallway. "For God's sake, Kirkpatrick, hurry!" he cried. "Order your men to clear the building. I tried to make them and they just giggled at me. Said you swore you'd kill the first man who let anyone out."

"I did!" Kirkpatrick snapped. "What the hell's the matter with you, Dick?"

"Ozone!" Wentworth flung at him. "The building's full of it!"

"It's from the fire." Kirkpatrick was growing angry, his hard cheeks flushed.

"Snap out of it, Kirk!" Wentworth cried. *"We're upwind from the fire!"* He abruptly brought the flat of his hand across Kirkpatrick's face.

Kirkpatrick staggered back under the blow. Scarlet stained his cheeks. His fists knotted. The sergeant leaped forward with his gun whipped up for a blow, and Wentworth stepped into his charge, drove his fist hard to the man's jaw and spun him back against the wall.

"Hurry, Kirk!" Wentworth pleaded. "Don't you understand, the Fairlands own this building, too? *At any minute, it will burst into flames!"*

CHAPTER EIGHT
The Tower of Flame!

ANGER still glinted in Kirkpatrick's eyes, but he held himself in check. He squeezed his eyes hard shut.

"Kirkpatrick!" Wentworth pleaded. "There isn't a moment to lose! There are thousands of people in this building. *Thousands!* We've got to clear them out, make sure no matches are struck, no guns fired, or this whole building—with all the human beings in it—will turn into a tower of flame!"

Kirkpatrick's arms swung down, his eyes peering deeply into Wentworth's.

"Thanks, Dick," he whispered. "Thanks. I know you're right now. The evidence was all around me, but . . ." His voice rose crisply, and thanksgiving flowed through Wentworth's veins as he heard the old confident energy in those tones.

"Sergeant!" Kirkpatrick cried. "Empty every office on this floor. Tell them the air is full of gas. If they strike a match, they'll blow up! If anybody starts to disobey, brain him! *But don't shoot!"*

The sergeant pushed groggily away from the wall, turned into the first office.

"A suggestion, Kirk," Wentworth said swiftly. "Open all windows and doors. You get down to the first floor and call more men here. Call fire equipment. Warn all offices immediately against smoking and get guards in all offices to enforce that. That's even more important than getting people moving out!"

Kirkpatrick nodded briskly. An elevator door popped open and he sprang into it. "I'll give you four elevators for this floor, Dick. Be with you as soon as I can. Down, man, down—and no stops!"

The door clanged shut, and Kirkpatrick was plunging earthward.

Wentworth spun toward the door through which the sergeant had run and there was no sign of exodus yet. Anger surged through his veins.

"Hold the next four cars that come to the top!" he snapped at the two uniformed men. "Pack them as full as rush-hour loads and order the operators not to stop until they reach the first floor. Then have them bounce back up here fast. And if you see anybody start to light a match, *hit him fast and hard!"*

He was running as he finished, shouting words over his shoulder. He had a gun in his hand and, when he reached the door through which the sergeant had gone, he smashed the glass from it, leveled the gun.

"Everybody out of here at once!" he shouted. He pointed the gun at two men who were arguing with the sergeant.

The two men stared in amazement but, at his repeated order, sidled forward in fright. "But my business!" one of them protested hoarsely. "I can't stop my whole force from working ...."

Wentworth struck him down with the gun barrel. "Everybody out!" he snapped. "Carry this man with you. The building is full of gas. If a match is struck, it will go up in flames and carry you with it—like the fire on Fifth Avenue! March!"

A girl uttered a little cry and darted for the door. "Don't run!" Wentworth snapped. "The elevators will be waiting for you. Sergeant, keep them moving. And break the skull of the first fool who tries to strike a match!"

WENTWORTH whirled and plunged to the next office. There was a fury in his veins. People were so slow to recognize what must be done! Even when it was life and death for themselves, they must stop and argue. He forced himself to be calm. He did realize that danger and sudden death were strangers to those who moved in ordinary walks of life. They did not have his quick and ready perception of peril, he who walked in deadly danger every day of his life!

Wentworth punched open the next door, kicked a stop to hold it open and smashed out the glass. A girl leaped to her feet with a small scream; the door of an inner private office whipped open.

"Out!" Wentworth called. "Everybody out at once. This is the police. This building is going up in flames!"

He had less trouble with this smaller force, designating two men to knock out all the windows. The cold breath of the northern gale whined into the room, sent papers flying. Snow made a pale white flickering against the black and red of the night.

The sergeant had stormed ahead to the next office and was profiting by Wentworth's example, working more quickly now.

"Smash out all windows," Wentworth threw at him as he ran past. "Open all doors. It may break down the gas somewhat. When you get the last ones off of this floor, order the elevators to take the third floor down!" As he ran past the bank of elevators, he picked up one of the uniformed men. "Come with me!"

Wentworth took the steps downward in great leaping strides. his mind racing like his legs. There were eighty stories in this giant sky-scraper. He shook his head in quick worry.

Wentworth skated out into the hall, ducked toward the first office door. "Come with me," he told the policeman with enforced calm. "Watch what I do, and when you understand, duck to the next office and do the same thing. There's no time for argument. If anyone tries to stop you, knock him down and have him carried out by those others. Understand?"

The man said grimly, "Yes, sir." He giggled. "Suppose they're all girls!"

Wentworth swung around and slapped the man hard across the face, twice. "You're drunk on oxygen!" he snapped. "Realize that and try to control yourself! Remember, a match or a gunshot means death for all of us. We'll catch fire like giant matches and flames will spurt out of our flesh!"

The man went pale under the lash of his words. "I'm sorry, sir," he whispered. "I'll brace up."

In less than thirty seconds Wentworth

had people started out of the office. The policeman pivoted on his heel and ran to the next door and an elevator clanged open to discharge three uniformed men. They strode up to Wentworth, though one of them staggered in his walk, and all had the flushed faces,

"Orders to report to you, sir," one of them mumbled.

With a jerk of his hand, Wentworth sent them into the first office, already emptied. "Get to the windows and suck in fresh air," he ordered. "When your heads are clear, come back. I may be on the floor below. You're useless to me as you are!"

He pounded toward the elevator. "Wait until you can't squeeze another person on. Empty on the first floor and shoot back up." The operator grinned vapidly, swaying on his feet, and Wentworth swore under his breath. No matter how rapidly the police worked, if the oxygen intoxication increased, the elevators would be stalled. Everything depended on getting fresh men here from headquarters at the first possible moment. Wentworth glanced at his watch. Seven minutes since he had entered the building! He had half emptied two floors! He groaned aloud.

One of the policemen strode to his side. His face was red with cold, but alertness was in his step. "I'm ready, sir," he said. "Get to the floor below," Wentworth ordered. "Run into every office and warn them that if anyone lights a match, they'll all burn to death. Make it strong. If you have an opportunity to knock somebody kicking, so much the better. They'll believe you, then. Warn them to be ready to leave the building, but don't make any violent attempt to get them in motion yet. I'll send more men to help you."

THE man sprang to the steps, and Wentworth sucked in a quicker breath of relief. The ozone was thicker here than it had been on the floor above and, though the fresh air pouring through the smashed windows helped some, Wentworth knew it would not prevent fire. The Flame Men had used their diabolical device in the open air in their attack on the banks!

Another of the policemen ran to him and Wentworth duplicated his instructions. "Smash windows, as you go," he directed, "but above all things, prevent anyone from striking a match!"

Only two offices remained to be emptied on this floor. Wentworth stood in the hallway, calmly. The elevators were pumping up and down regularly, but the crowd eddied into the corridors more swiftly than they could be moved on. Wentworth's eyes flicked over them inceasingly. He saw a man covertly tuck a cigarette into his mouth, tear a match from a booklet. With two leaping strides, Wentworth was upon him. His fist lashed out savagely, and the man stretched his length on the floor.

The beginning of panic rippled through the crowd. A few pivoted and darted for the stairs. "Come back!" Wentworth called, keeping his voice smooth with an effort. "The elevators will be faster. You'll all get out all right, if you'll just be calm—*and don't smoke!*"

An elevator spilled out three more policemen, and they ran up to Wentworth. With a sense of relief that was almost prayer, Wentworth saw that they were fresh and unaffected by the gas. Probably new men, or some pulled in from outside posts. With crisp words, he explained the situation, sent them to warn floors below about matches or smoking.

"Commissioner says he'll be with you in a few minutes, sir," one reported.

The sergeant who had been working above came into the hallway at a dead run. "Top floor clear!" he reported. "Sent the elevators to the floor below this one!"

"Get down there!" Wentworth ordered. "You'll find the people prepared, but not moving yet. Good work, Sergeant."

The man wheeled and raced down stairs. People were streaming from the last offices on this floor. Wentworth kept one officer to help him keep guard against fools who would strike matches in defiance of reason and orders, sent the other to lower floors.

He could feel the exhilaration of the oxygen pumping out from his lungs. His fists were knotted with the effort to keep his brain clear. In the back of that brain was the nagging thought that he was overlooking something, that he was making a serious error. The idea was there, but he could not bring it to light. Laboriously, while he herded the office workers into elevators, he went over the work they were doing, point by point. Where was his mistake? What had he failed to do? They seemed to be covering every possible point, getting people out swiftly, combatting everything that might start a fire ....

Abruptly, Wentworth stepped back, dazed with the suddenness of realization. After making elaborate preparations to destroy the building, would the Master leave the fuse to chance? Would he depend on an opportune match, or would he ... make sure! But Wentworth knew the answer even as he phrased it in his own mind. The Master would *make sure!* But how? No way of guessing that. Twice previously, he had provoked an answering gunfire to touch off the flames ....

The last of the crowd was jamming into an elevator. Wentworth seized the remaining policeman by the shoulders.

"Report to Kirkpatrick," he ordered, "or whomever is in command on the main floor . . . *Hold that elevator, boy! . . . .* I think *some one from outside* may try to start the fire. Better surround the building with a guard, but order them not to shoot! Tell Kirkpatrick that from me!"

HE thrust the officer into the elevator. When the door slammed shut, Wentworth leaned against it. The cold night wind whined through the corridors. Where a window gave jaggedly on the night, he could glimpse the whirling snow, now white from the lights within, now red with the glare of the burning railway terminal. Heaven grant that he had thought of that in time!

But he could not delay here. There was more work below stairs, more people to herd into elevators and safety. Now the ozone seemed denser. Wentworth's step faltered as he turned toward the stairs. He fought down a surging impulse to laughter. Drunk! Drunk on oxygen... and only two floors had been emptied!

As he moved with enforced steadiness down the steps, he caught the sounds of shouts and laughter; the senseless high giggles of women, men's guffaws. He sprang out into the hallway, but found the sergeant had this floor well under control. The racket, like the bedlam of a drunken party, came from below.

Wentworth hailed two policemen and raced on down. Twice, he stumbled and barely saved himself with grabbing hands. He shouldered out through the door. Waves of sound beat upon him. The corridor was jammed with reeling men and women. An elevator door slammed, and the operator yelled, but no one heeded him.

A girl caught hold of his arm. "Come

on and dance. Nobody's going down!"

The operator grinned and started out, and Wentworth fought his way through the mëlée, slammed the man back into the cage, thrust the girl after him. He wasted no words on ears that would not hear, but tumbled others unceremoniously into the cage. In a moment, the two police were helping him.

A man and woman danced without music. Wentworth seized the girl and whirled her through the elevator doors, strode toward the man. His heavy red face was scowling. With a curse, he charged and swung his hamlike fists. Wentworth's feet were uncertain. He stumbled, and a fist caught him high on the cheek-bone, hammered him backward. Hell, he couldn't let them start fighting! He and his men would be overwhelmed in an instant, and then . .. death for all!

The man was charging in again, shouting now. Wentworth retreated, stumbling dazedly and got his back to the elevator. As the man rushed, he managed to step aside, sent him reeling in.

"Down!" Wentworth gasped at the operator. "Take them down!"

The door slammed and Wentworth pushed through the drunken crowd. "Smash windows!" he called hoarsely to his two men. "Smash windows, and get some air through here!"

Wentworth just made a window. When he had driven an elbow through the pane, he leaned there, drinking in cold drafts of the night wind. He shivered uncontrollably. The task was hopeless, completely hopeless. Impossible to work in this dense concentration of oxygen and keep a clear head; impossible to move drunken mobs with any celerity. But it must be done.

Wentworth spun from the window, almost cried aloud with joy at his renewed strength. In the hallway, people were huddling together under the lash of the cold winds. Another elevator flung open its doors, and this time they wedged into it without urging. When the next cage came up, Kirkpatrick stepped out. He strode toward Wentworth with relief shining in his eyes.

"Time to go, old man," he said softly. "Things are organized as well as possible. I've got at least one man on every floor and more are coming. Another twenty minutes and we'll have most of them out."

"Twenty minutes!" Wentworth echoed dully. Twenty thousand opportunities for sudden, overwhelming disaster!

THE elevator had filled and still other people fought to enter. The two uniformed men shouldered in, slammed the doors. A tall, dark-faced man spun and struck down with his fists, drove a cop to the floor. As suddenly as that, the riot started. Men and women screamed and beat at the two officers . . . and time was speeding, speeding toward death!

Instantly, Wentworth and Kirkpatrick sprang into the thick of it, lashed out with their guns. The riot broke as quickly as it had started and Wentworth helped the battered policeman to his feet. One arm dangled limply. Kirkpatrick swore.

"You'll walk down, now!" he shouted bitterly at the crowd. "And I'll shoot the first man who runs!" He singled out the one who had started the riot. "You'll go last! March!"

Wailing, the crowd moved slowly toward the stairs.

Kirkpatrick said somberly, "Dick, we've got to get out. This oxygen is beginning to get me again."

An elevator door clanged, and Kirkpatrick strode toward it. "Come on,

Dick."

Wentworth shook his head, "You're needed on the first floor, Kirk. I'm needed here. I'll follow the men down, floor by floor."

For a long moment, Kirkpatrick glowered at him. There was the whiteness of muscle tension along his jaw, but he made his lips smile abruptly. He whirled on the elevator man. And his words cut keenly.

"What are you waiting for?" he snapped. "Get going. Two floors below this one." Kirkpatrick turned to Wentworth. "I still think this is madness. It's almost impossible to get everyone out. Your life is too valuable to risk."

Wentworth turned toward the stairs. So long as they could prevent any spark of flame, the building was safe. Safe? Wentworth laughed aud the sound was crazy in his own ears. He felt Kirkpatrick's hand clamp down hard on his arm and choked off the sound. They must remain calm, prevent any panic.

He made his walk a stroll, as they turned into the hallway of the floor below. The last huddle of people was waiting for an elevator, wide-eyed and frightened. There was tension in the poise of the single policeman with them, too. At sight of Kirkpatrick and Wentworth, strolling, talking quietly together, his tension eased. He did not notice the locked rigidity of Wentworth's jaw.

"You can go to the next floor, officer," Wentworth drawled. "These people are all right. We'll see them off."

The man saluted smartly and walked quietly toward the steps. Wentworth apparently ignored the crowd, but Kirkpatrick's eyes were sharply on them, watching for the danger of a match. As they filed into an elevator, Wentworth flung a hand in farewell and walked toward the stairs, downward again.

Kirkpatrick said, "Five of the twenty minutes I allotted are gone."

In the next corridor the sergeant came up to them briskly, but his stride was irregular and his face highly flushed.

"I got windows smashed for five floors below," he reported. "We're working in relays."

Kirkpatrick nodded casually. "Good work, Sergeant. Carry on."

"The open windows aren't helping," Wentworth said softly, "except that the men can revive a little when they are alongside them. It seems to me that the oxygen is actually denser where windows are open."

An elevator brought a policeman who came up to Kirkpatrick at a run. "Machine guns opened fire on the guard outside, sir, and no one can get out of the building," he whispered. "We turned a hose on them. Inspector Hardy says to tell you he took ammunition away from all our men."

Kirkpatrick's jaw set rigidly. "That's massacre," he said hoarsely. He glanced at his watch. "We've got to smash a way through, or else..."

"Inspector Hardy wants you down there, sir!" the officer reported.

Kirkpatrick began to shake his head, but Wentworth thrust him toward the elevator. "You're needed Kirk! For God's sake, go!"

Kirkpatrick turned, so swiftly that Wentworth did not guess his purpose. He glimpsed the knotted fist too late to dodge and his senses blacked out. He came to quickly, to find hintself being walked through the first floor lobby toward the exit. All lights were out, and the rattle of machine guns was unceasing. He dug in his feet.

"I'm going back!" he said violently. Kirkpatrick spun on him. "You're going with me, Dick," he said harshly, "or I'll put you in handcuffs. Stop being a fool!"

Wentworth felt anger hot and brassy in his throat, scarcely hearing the words that Kirkpatrick continued to hurl at him.

"It isn't necessary for you to prove your courage, Dick!" Kirkpatrick was saying. "Foolhardiness is not courage. If you are killed up there, *who will find the Master?* Dick, listen to me. You're drunk on oxygen!"

Wentworth drew in a slow, quivering breath. An interne stepped toward him at Kirkpatrick's signal and jerked up his sleeve, dug a hypodermic into his flesh. Afterward, Wentworth's head felt clearer.

"All right, Kirk," he said quietly. "You win. I'll see what we can do to break up this attack!"

HE looked about him. The main lobby was jammed with people, and more were pouring out of the elevators every moment, but the welter of lead that screamed outside penned them in. Wentworth crept toward the doors and peered out. Three machine guns were firing in short bursts from the corners of buildings. Their slugs rained across the doorway, dug into the walls, screamed as they ricocheted from the pavement.

"God, Kirk!" he whispered. "Suppose they fired . . . *tracers!* It would only take one phosphorous bullet to touch off the fire!"

With the words, he flung himself prone on the pavement and crawled out. "Stay inside!" he called softly. "I can do this alone!"

The curb was banked solid with police cars and ambulances. The snow swept in stinging sheets along the canyon of the street. He saw three policemen stretched dead on the pavement and at the thought of their empty guns, Wentworth swore fiercely under his breath. It was only a question of time before tracer fire was directed on the building. The Master was too clever not to think of that when his effort to provoke return fire had failed.

Wentworth reached the curb and wriggled out between two cars to a third that was parked beyond them. The machine guns were hammering from two directions—from the ends of the opposite block. Wentworth crawled over the runningboard, still in the protection of the car, crouched on the floor. He dared not start the engine lest a backfire touch off the conflagration, but the car was parked on a slight grade. He eased the brakes and, still on the floor, put one hand on the wheel.

Slowly, the coupe gathered headway. Lead hammered across the hood, dropped the windshield across his back in fragments. A tire went out with a hissing blast. The car trundled on. Only Wentworth's left hand, gripping the steering wheel, was exposed to gunfire.

He drew an automatic with his right, and waited. It was plain that the machine gunners were beyond the ignition point of the chemical. When Wentworth reached their vicinity, he would be, too. He could shoot then . . . if they did not get him first. Two machine guns on opposite sides of the street would have him in a deadly cross-fire. For the present, he was protected by the thickness of the metal in the engine, but these flimsy sheetsteel sides would not shield him then.

Water from a hose swished across the coupe, struck its rear and made it roll more rapidly down the street, and Wentworth laughed softly. Kirkpatrick had guessed his plan and was speeding him on his way! Wentworth dared a quick glance above the cowling, twisted the steering wheel and headed straight for the nearest machine gunner! The coupe jarred over the curbing, trundled along the sidewalk. Twenty-five feet to go, now fifteen.

The hammer of lead was unceasing. The car shook under the storm of bullets, shuddered, but the pressure from behind, and gravity, urged it on. There would be a moment when the car grazed past the corner that the machine gunner would be driven from his post. He need only step backward and keep the bullets coming, but he was hammering out lead in a frenzy. At that speed, it would take only moments to empty the machine gun's drum. Then he must detach it, slap another into place. And then ....

The coupe scraped against the corner of the building. There was a lull in the gunfire. Wentworth popped up, gun and head only, and glimpsed a man backing away. Wentworth squeezed out a single shot and ducked down again. He heard a scream. Instantly, Wentworth punched open the door and slid head-first to the pavement. From beneath the car, he could see the dark form of the second gunner as he pumped lead into the coupe. He drew a careful bead, and once more the automatic spoke.

The flicker of flame from the machine gun swung in an erratic arc, then blotted out. It clattered on the pavement and the dark form of the gunman pitched across it. Wentworth sprang back into the car, groped for the key. The starter whirred... then the motor coughed into life.

Instantly, Wentworth had the machine moving. The engine sputtered and shook in its mountings. The bullets from the machine guns had done their work, but he need only travel a short way— around the block—and he could take the third machine gunner from the rear.

The car seemed barely to crawl. Wentworth laughed softly to himself. He had been right about one thing. The Master's forces were depleted, and apparently he had not yet recruited fresh men.

Wentworth rounded the first corner. A man in the middle of the street began to shoot, trying to pull his machine gun on the target. Wentworth let his automatic fall into line and fired once. It was enough. When he rounded the next corner, he could see no flicker of gunfire. Evidently, that guard had fled his post when his companions' weapos were silenced. Yes, there were the first of the escaping horde from the building. They filled the street from wall to wall, surging frantically away from the spire that might at any moment burst into flame.

WENTWORTH ran the coupe to the curb and jumped to the street. Along the wall, he began to fight his way back toward the building. The Keystone Spire must be almost clear. Once the structure was empty, they could wash it with high-pressure hoses and perhaps dissipate the chemical. But he'd have to reach Kirkpatrick at once. He ....

A wailing scream swept the fleeing mob. A gust of titanic proportions picked up men and women and tossed them like sticks. It ground Wentworth against the wall where he fought, deafened him, blotted out all senses save vision. On its heels, came fire. A vast roiling cloud of flame swept once over the heads of the multitude. It leaned out over the crests of buildings and licked its hot tongues down from above. Suddenly it was gone, sucked up toward the heavens.

The Keystone Spire, towering a thousand feet straight up into the air, became a gigantic torch. Over all its length the very stone spouted streams of crimson and gold. They curled around it, spiraled and danced, merged into a gargantuan spear-head of flame that seemed to pierce the heavens. It dazzled the eyes like sunlight. Wentworth felt the up-sucking draft drag at him like living hands.

He saw one, a dozen men swept backward and up into the heart of the holocaust, tossed like bits of burning paper, their screams thin and empty in the vast, overwhelming voice of the flames. Up the street swept the remnants of the fugitive horde, making faint wailing sounds that were like the piping of fleeing mice. And over it all, the heat struck like a hammer. Wentworth turned heavily to follow the retreat, and his strength was faint in his limbs, his lungs scorched. A woman's dress burst into flame, and Wentworth flung his overcoat to smother the fire.

Instantly, the heat searched him out and beat upon his flesh. He worked toward the farther side of the street, where rising walls might offer some protection from the direct rays, shouted vain words at the fleeing horde. They didn't hear him, couldn't. They were blind and deaf with terror. They ran with wide open eyes that could not see. For blocks, that blind stampede fought on against the rushing draft. And finally, the dark streets absorbed them, the snow which for hundreds of feet was wiped out by the heat, swirled about them like a kindly shroud.

Wentworth set his shoulders against a wall and panted and groaned aloud. Kirkpatrick had stayed behind in the building!

CHAPTER NINE
Clue of Doom

FOR moments that were like hours, Wentworth stood staring at the flames which, he felt, had made the funeral pyre of his friend. When he turned away, his face was drawn into line of suffering. Rage ate at his heart. Some such end as this inevitably waited for them both, death in the line of duty. Neither could hope to escape.

Wentworth swore no oath, but in his heart was the grim determination that before another sun arose, the Master should pay! Heaven alone knew how many brave men had died in the holocaust of the Keystone Spire ....

Wentworth pulled up sharply and realized that he was shivering with cold. He dimly remembered using his overcoat to snuff burning clothes. His hat was long since gone, and the snow whipped against him. He thought of calling Jackson or Ram Singh—and he remembered both were incapacitated. He flung into a late-closing clothing store and, while coats and hats were brought forward, put in a call for headquarters. No report of Kirkpatrick since the fire, but there had been two calls from Miles Scott ....

"I'll be there in fifteen minutes," Wentworth snapped. "If he calls again, please get the number."

He seized the first dark coat that was offered him, jerked a slouch hat on his brows and flung money on the counter, strode out into the night. A taxi waited, and he sent it skittering southward toward Centre Street. "Forget the speed limits," Wentworth rasped. "This is police business."

It did not even seem strange to Wentworth that the *Spider* should give such orders. Actually, he held a special deputy's badge which Kirkpatrick had given him

The Keystone spire, towering a thousand feet up into the air, became a gigantic torch.

long ago in some half-remembered battle when they had fought shoulder to shoulder. And tonight, Kirkpatrick had authorized headquarters to take his orders over the phone. Wentworth was thinking he might be able to utilize these orders— if Kirkpatrick were missing. He might get away with it for a few hours, until the truth was known and the first deputy succeeded to Kirkpatrick's powers.

Wentworth had not yet mapped a plan of action, but he was determined that this night should see the end of the Master! Miles Scott's calls set his mind racing back to the scene in the office before the fire alarm had hit. Miles had heard the details on the phone call Doña Margherita had made, and the fact that she was believed to be speaking to Don Carlos. It was only a jump from that to guess that Beulah might be in the same place. Wentworth hoped nothing had happened to the youth.

The taxi slued to a halt before headquarters, and Wentworth started somberly up the steps. His step was almost buoyant when he paced through the bright entrance foyer, circled up the wide steps toward the commissioner's office.

Kirkpatrick's secretary met him at the door, asked rapidly for the commissioner.

"He's at the scene of the fire," Wentworth told him shortly. "I want the reports I asked for over the phone. If Miles Scott calls again, have the call put directly through to me. Get the Spanish Consulate on the wire. I want to speak with Miss van Sloan."

His easy assumption of authority got results, and he went directly into the barren, big office of Kirkpatrick. Almost, he expected to find his saturnine friend behind the desk. His eyes went there subconsciously as he hooked his hat and coat on the rack.

His thoughts were cut short by the whirring of the phone, and he crossed to it rapidly. Nita's clear rich voice came to him, and Wentworth's taut face softened.

"Dick," Nita whispered. "Dick, I'm... afraid here. No, there's no reason for it that I know, but I am!"

Wentworth questioned her quickly, and apprehension gripped him anew. Like himself, Nita had lived too long in the heart of peril to be foolishly frightened.

"Why not leave there?" he asked. "Go to my home."

"Are you quitting the fight, Dick?" Nita asked dryly, and Wentworth knew there was no use in further protest. His heart was in his grave, deep voice. "All right, dearest, but guard yourself! If anything should happen to you .... "

"*Sssh,*" Nita interrupted. "Listen to this. Margherita told me that note was a ransom letter from kidnapers and that she was allowed to speak to Don Carlos. They're demanding a half million!"

Wentworth's eyes narrowed. "Think that's the truth?" he asked.

"I don't know, Dick," Nita told him, "but there is no doubt that Margherita is terribly worried. I know she called Tavish and asked him if he could raise the money. I've got to go now."

Nita hung up before Wentworth could speak again. His head jerked up as Kirkpatrick's secretary came in with a batch of reports. "Here's the data on the Fairland holdings," he said. "And on Tavish and the other men of the board of directors. We've only been able to reach two of the heirs. Here's what they say."

Wentworth ran his eyes swiftly down the sheets and he felt new tension grip him. Both of the heirs reported offers from Humboldt Tavish for their stock in the holding company! And on Wall Street, Fairland steamship stock was tumbling and being purchased in huge blocks by that same investment company! Wentworth rose to his feet.

"I'll call in later," he told the secretary. "Be sure you have Miles Scott leave a number, and ...."

The phone buzzed as he reached for his coat, and he reached it in a bound. "This is Wentworth speaking," he said swiftly. and frowned as he recognized Scott's voice. "Where are you, Scott?"

Scott was whispering swiftly, "Thank God, I've reached you at last! Listen, I'm sure Beulah is hidden here. Yes, at the beer parlor. Can you come?"

"In five minutes!" Wentworth snapped. Tavish could wait.

TWO minutes later, he sprang into a taxi at the door and sent it hurtling toward the Bowery and Chatham Square. The beer saloon called Frank's Place was a dim-lighted hole. It had a furtive, ugly air.

Wentworth turned up the collar of his coat and was glad that the new hat was cheap and soaked by melting snow. His whole manner changed in the half-dozen strides that carried him to the door of the saloon. Gone was his erect, challenging stride, and in its place was a man of stooped shoulders and shuffling gait. The very lines of his face changed and sagged with despondency. It was one of the secrets of Wentworth's superlative capacity for disguise that he became utterly, even physically, the person whose character he assumed.

He slouched up to the bar and, in a snuffling, whining voice asked for whisky. It was a tribute to his powers that the barman waited until he laid money on the counter before he obeyed the order. There was a scattering of men in the place and, eyes shuttling under the drawn-down brim of his hat, Wentworth quickly spotted Miles Scott, leaning over a glass of beer at a corner table. Scott's eyes were fixed on Wentworth, but presently they dropped again to his beer, without recognizing him.

Wentworth frowned. It seemed incredible that Miles Scott could have remained here for the length of time he had without being spotted as a spy—that is, if this place really were a hangout of the Master's men. Perhaps he had, and was being watched in turn. That meant Wentworth, too, would fall under suspicion the moment he approached Scott. Deliberately, Wentworth thumbed his hat back from his forehead, took a second drink while he watched in the fly-specked mirror. As soon as he was sure Scott had spotted him, he jerked his hat down and shuffled out. In a matter of moments, Scott followed.

"Thank God, you've come!" he whispered. "Listen, I've seen fifteen men go upstairs and not one of them has come back down again. Once, I saw the same man come in again from the street, but I'll swear he didn't go out through the saloon. There must be another entrance, or maybe a secret connection with another building. There's a big loft building over behind here, tenements on each side. And listen, at least ten of those men were real Spaniards!"

Wentworth was gazing beyond Scott, into the darkness. He had seen two men ease out of a tenement doorway and they were stealing forward now. Wentworth's lips thinned in a smile. Only one thing made a gleam like that which came from their right hands, the blue steel of guns! Without a word, Wentworth swung his right leg in a sweeping arc, knocked Scott's legs out from under him. Wentworth flung himself down. At the same moment, his guns leaped to his hand.

Even as they fell, gun-flame slashed at them. Wentworth fired two deliberate shots and was instantly on his feet.

"Sorry, Scott," he whispered, "it was the only way. Come on!"

Without a second glance at the two men his bullets had blown down, Wentworth led a dash for the doorway from which they had stepped. Before men from the saloon could reach the exit, Wentworth and Scott were within the dark doorway, and Wentworth led the way up the decrepit stairs. He shouted, and made his voice hoarse.

"They are dead!" he cried in Spanish, "but we are pursued. Open the door!"

A door dead ahead flung open, and a man was outlined against brilliant light. Behind him, another door stood open, leading into what seemed a closet, but which had a second door beyond that gave on a long corridor. Wentworth saw tension grip the man in the doorway, saw him start backward into the room, dragging at a gun. Wentworth dared not risk another shot now. With a quick whip of his forearm, he hurled his automatic. It glanced from the man's temple, sent him reeling. Before he could recover, Wentworth had slashed through the doorway and his fist had finished the job. He caught up his automatic.

"No time to tie him up," he whispered. "He'll keep for a half hour now! We'll have to work fast. Before the men in the saloon know who's dead and phone up their report!"

IN a moment, he was through the closet and had closed both doors behind them. He delayed to discover the operating mechanism of the secret entrance, then dashed on. He made no effort at silence, for those within would be expecting the return of the assassins. His eyes quested ahead, and each hand held an automatic.

Wentworth motioned Scott up beside him. "This is the loft building, all right," he said. "Your guess was entirely correct. I don't know what we'll find behind the door at the head of those steps ahead, but whatever happens will be fast. Have you got a gun?"

Scott nodded.

"Good," Wentworth said curtly. "I'm going to punch open that door and jump through. If you stand right behind me, you'll be hit by return fire. Squeeze up against one wall, crouch low and don't shoot fast. Make sure of your target before you let go. Understand?"

They were running up the stairs now. Wentworth grabbed the knob, wrenched it and sprang through in a long leap.

Two men were sprawled over a table scattered with playing cards. Their eyes popped wide, and one grabbed for a gun. Before he could bring it into play, Wentworth was upon them. His automatic whipped down on the head of the first, sideways against the temple of the second, and the two men were out.

"Hell," Scott said, "you don't need me! I'm just excess ...." He choked off then, whirled toward a door to his right. From behind it, a woman's voice called again. "Miles! Oh, Miles ...."

Miles Scott flung himself at the barrier, wrenched at the knob.

Wentworth smiled and ran quickly through the pockets of the unconscious man, stepped to Scott's side. "Why not use a key?" he asked gently.

Scott stepped back, his face flushed, and Wentworth worked the lock. In a moment, Scott had bounded through and flung himself down beside a bed to which Beulah Loraine was tied, hand and foot.

Wentworth remained outside. There

was a second door in the room, and he opened it quicky and stepped through. Fragments of rope lay on the floor. Don Carlos, or someone else, had been held a prisoner here, but was gone now. A door in the room opened on a vast room into which street-lights filtered dimly. There seemed to be a fire exit on the far side. Wentworth hurried back to Scott and the girl.

"No time to lose," he said swiftly. "That mob downstairs will be here in two minutes. Follow me!"

THE girl staggered on her feet, and Scott canght her up in his arms, ran heavy-footed where Wentworth pointed. Wentworth delayed long enough to lock all doors, then sped across the dim loft room to the fire-exit door, knocked up the bar that held it and led the way down stairs. A few moments later, they slid out into the dark street that paralleled the Bowery. Scott had thrown his coat about Beulah's shoulders, and she was staggering along beside him now.

It was four blocks before they found a taxi. Once inside, Wentworth turned to the girl.

"When you went into the consulate the other night, you saw a fat-faced man," he said rapidly. "You were frightened. Why?"

Beulah stared up at him with large startled eyes, and Miles Scott rattled words at her, telling who Wentworth was.

Beulah shuddered. "I remember now!" she said. "Maybe it was silly of me, but when that poor man burst into flame, I saw that fat-faced one in the window. He laughed and rubbed his hands."

Wentworth leaned back against the cushions, "Thank you, my dear," he said softly. "Driver, when you spot another cab, stop beside it. Scott, Beulah is scarcely safe at home after this. Take her to the consulate, and Miss van Sloan will look after her. After tonight ...."

Miles Scott was staring at him. "You think Tavish ...." he began.

Wentworth shrugged. "Beulah, did you see Don Carlos—the Spanish consul, you remember—while you were a prisoner?"

"I think so, Mr. Wentworth," the girl said clearly. "A little while after I was kidnapped and taken to that place, three men brought in another one who was cursing at them in Spanish. As well as I remember, it was the same one who was at the consulate."

Wentworth nodded, gave the driver money as the cab stopped beside another. "You two go to the consulate and tell Miss van Sloan that I'll see her tonight."

Scott started to babble thanks, but Wentworth sprang into the other cab and flung his home address at the man. Tavish's home was on the upper East Side. In a short while, he would receive a call from the *Spider!* The man must talk... Until the secrets of the Flame were learned, and the entire organization dispersed, there could be no safety for the millions. The terror of the *Spider* had often helped to loosen men's tongues!

THE taxi drew to the curb before an apartment house on Sutton Place which Wentworth had purchased. He entered the suite on the first floor, went hurriedly through it and into a bedroom closet. A touch on a secret spring, and the wall opened, revealing stairs and, below, a lighted concrete tunnel. Through this, Wentworth hurried, and pressed a hidden spring. The ceiling opened downward and the cage of the elevator of his home slid downward. Moments later, Wentworth was stepping into the drawing-room of his home.

Jackson stepped forward, saluted with his left hand, his right arm in splints and a sling. "I've had calls from Miss Nita and from a Miles Scott," he reported laconicaly. "Last one an hour ago."

Wentworth nodded, "I made contact. How's Ram Singh?"

Jackson's wide mouth grinned briefly. "Wants to get up and fight. I had to threaten to clout him. Major, I want to apologize..."

"Forget it," Wentworth said. "I'm sorry I had to break your arm. Tonight, Jackson, the *Spider* walks. Could you handle the car in an emergency?"

"Try me, sir!" Jackson snapped. "Stand by for a call, then."

He went striding to his bedroom, through it into his elaborate bath, whose walls were mosaic tile. He stepped up to a design of centaurs and touched certain tiles in sequence. A narrow door swung open and he stepped through—into a complete dressing-room where racks of clothing hung and where a dressing-table, whose mirror was ringed with neon tubes, provided every possible article of disguise and make-up. Ten minutes later, he reentered the elevator.

"I'm taking the Daimler," he said. "If I call you, get a car from the garage that uses an electric gear-shift. That will be easier for you. Better have the car ready."

Jackson's eyes were fixed on his disguised face—the lipless, sinister face of the *Spider.* "Major, let me go with you."

Wentworth shook his head, sent the elevator down. He took a cross-tunnel, whose hidden entrance lay in the one by which he had first entered. A few moments later, the doors of a private garage on the sidestreet swung open and a black limousine glided, almost noiselessly, out onto the snow-carpeted street.

It was twenty minutes later that the same car slid to the curb near an apartment house in the East Eighties. The shadows received another darker shadow that moved on soundless feet and crept into the trade entrance of the building. Swift, expert fingers picked the lock of the door and the shadow that was the *Spider* moved on, up the enclosed fire stairway to the eighteenth floor. A sliver of spring steel forced the catch of the door and he was in the corridor before the penthouse of Humboldt Tavish!

A red spot of fury burned in the *Spider's* brain. Behind these doors was the man who, he was certain now, had loosed the terror of the Flame upon the city; the man who was responsible for death after death, and Kirkpatrick . . . . Wentworth had to enter this apartment, make Tavish talk and then... the seal of the *Spider* would claim its own!

He bent before the door and studied the lock for an instant, then slid a slender steel probe from a leather girdle about his waist. A few moments of work, a subdued click, and the door swung silently open under the *Spider's* hand. He closed it behind him, listening tensely. He could hear stumbling footsteps off to the left.

On fleet, silent feet, he sped along the corridor that stretched that way, peered into a room lighted by a single lamp. A curse rose in his throat. He sprang in and seized a man who crouched over . .. *the dead body of Humboldt Tavish!*

THERE was no resistance in the man Wentworth seized. The gun wrenched easily free into his hand, and he flung the man into a deep chair, staring into the frightened, white face of—Miles Scott!

"Oh God," Scott moaned. "Don't kill me, *Spider!* I swear to you I didn't kill Tavish! I swear I didn't!"

Wentworth's llps were slitted together, his eyes probing into the terrorized face of Miles Scott. Wentworth was trembling with anger, with frustration. He had come here to force from Tavish truths upon which a thousand lives depended, and this young fool ....

"I didn't do it, *Spider!*" Scott insisted. "I came up here to beat hell out of him for what he did to my girl friend. Somebody said over the phone to come up. The door was standing open, and, when I walked in, he was lying there dead!"

Wentworth fought for clear thought. If only he had not stopped to don the disguise of the *Spider,* he would have got here ahead of Scott. Wentworth lifted the captured gun to his nostrils in sudden doubt. The gun had not been fired! Then Scott told the truth. But, if that was so, *who was the Flame Master?*

Abruptly, Wentworth whirled about. The front doorbell was ringing, and someone was beating hard on the door! With long strides, Wentworth moved toward it.

"Crash the door!" a man ordered. "We've got him surrounded. He can't get away! Go on, I order you to do it. You damned dumb cops, get busy!"

Wentworth straightened and whisked back to the study where Tavish lay dead. "The police are at the door," he said curtly. "Come with me!"

He caught Scott by the arm, whipped him through to the terrace. He was unreeling a length of slender silken cord from a pocket of the cape.

"It's your only chance to get away," he said curtly. "I'11 swing you over the side. When you come to a dark window, kick it in and lie low. For God's sake, don't do any more meddling!"

Scott hesitated on the brink. His face was pale. "I'm not afraid," he said, "but what are you going to do, *Spider?* I'll swear to you ...."

Wentworth looped the line under the boy's shoulders. "Over with you!" he urged. "The snow will keep you from being seen. When you reach a dark window, hit the line with your fist. I'll feel it." Wentworth braced his feet, and began to pay Scott out over the edge of the terrace. His mind was whirling. What, exactly, did Tavish's death mean? All evidence pointed to him as the Flame Master. Damn it, he *had* to be guilty!

He felt a jar on the line and held it steady. A few moments later, it went limp and he hauled it in rapidly, 1ooping it into the pocket of his cape as he ran back to the study where Tavish lay.

Down the hall, a heavy weight was jarring against the door. Wentworth crouched and studied the bullet wound in Tavish's head. No, not suicide. There were no powder burns. Murder .... but by whom? He believed Scott's story ...

He ducked out into the corridor and crouched beside the door. Rapidly, he unscrewed a light bulb and touched the socket with the muzzle of his automatic. There was a blue-white flash of light and the entire apartment went dark. He had blown out a main fuse. The door was shaking in its socket now. On the next blow, it dynamited in, torn loose from its hinges, and a stream of men poured in ....

IN darkest shadow, crouched the Spider, a totally black figure. Men poured through the open door. One guard was left to watch. A moment after the policemen disappeared along the hallway, Wentworth sprang into action. His punch snapped out the man's senses like a light and, within seconds, the *Spider* was speeding down the fire stairs. When he sprang out on the first floor, two policemen whirled, their guns ready. Wentworth's leap blurred in its speed. The guns crashed, but futilely, at the floor. Wentworth struck twice with his own guns and was leaping out the exit. But when he sprang to the seat of the car, a gun was crashing at him from the corner. As he got under way, a siren began to whine. It took him a half hour of furious doubling through streets slippery with snow, but finally it was done.

And Wentworth had used the time to good advantage. He knew now what course he would follow. With the knowledge of Tavish's death, he could force Doña Margherita to tell the truth. He could scarcely have been involved in the work of the Flame Men without her knowledge. And she would talk! But he must have the chance to surprise her with the information. Miles Scott! By the heavens, the young fool would go rushing back to the consulate. He could have left the building a long while ago, for the *Spider* had drawn off the police, had taken the blame for the murder.

Furiously, Wentworth ripped off the disguise, and flung into a drugstore to use the phone. Nita would have to see that Scott didn't reach Margherita with the news, and then . . .

"Nita?" Wentworth's voice crackled with speed. "Tavish is dead ...."

"Miles Scott told us," Nita said swiftly. "And I think Margherita knows a lot and is willing to talk. I'm working on her and as soon as she gets over the first shock of grief, we can get it. You come here as quickly as you can. And, listen, Dick! Margherita says that the Flame Master is planning to loot the entire city tonight! Yes, that's what she says. I know it sounds fantastic, but with that flame...."

"I'll be there in fifteen minutes," Wentworth clipped out.

He spun from the booth and raced to his car. Confound that young fool, Scott! A brave kid, of course, but he had spoiled Wentworth's plans. Perhaps not, if Margherita would talk .... Wentworth bore the accelerator to the floor, sent the great black car roaring southward. A plan to loot the entire city, tonight. An exaggeration, of course, but if he struck at the financial district alone, he could seize millions, millions! Savagely, Wentworth fought the heavy Daimler over the slippery streets.

A tortured cry rose in Wentworth's throat. Rising, leaping against the southern skyline was the lurid glow of ... *fire!* Dear God, it couldn't be the consulate. It couldn't! Curses squeeezd out between Wentworth's teeth. He was denying what he knew to be the truth. It was the consulate!

Wentworth wrenched the Daimler to a halt, sprang to the street just short of the fire equipment that filled it from curb to curb. In a frenzy, he dashed toward the consulate, but while he was still a hundred yards away, the awful heat battered him to a halt. A hand closed on his arm, whirled him hack.

"For God's sake, you fool!" a man

said irritably, then he saw Wentworth's face, recognized him. "I'm sorry, Mr. Wentworth. I didn't know you."

Wentworth recognized Chief Dogan, seized him by the arms. "The people inside there, man. Tell me, what happened!"

Chief Dogan's eyes fell before the assault of Wentworth's glare. "The place was in flames when we got here." "But the people inside!"

Dogan shook his head. "We heard... screams. I'm afraid they are all..."

Wentworth staggered backward. His face twisted. "Dead?" he whispered. "All . . . *dead?*" he trembled. And slowly, the twisted horror left his face, brought a new, terrible expression in its place. He turned and ran furiously, blindly, into the night, and Chief Dogan shook himself, shuddered.

"Hell!" he whispered. "Hell, I'd hate to . . . to get in that man's way ...."

He was still muttering to himself as he moved on.

CHAPTER TEN
When Hell Broke Through!

POLICE headquarters was going mad. Its entire bureau of twenty-four telephone operators was sending out a series of frantic calls. The radio yammered unceasingly.

In the midst of the frenzy of activity, Commissioner Kirkpatrick walked in the front door. A sergeant, passing through the main corridor at a dead run, skidded, stumbled to a halt.

"Now glory be to God!" he stammered. "It's yourself, Commissioner!"

Kirkpatrick was in a savage humor, "Who else would it be?" he snapped and strode up the stairs, went charging into his office. His secretary uttered a stifled yelp, and Deputy Hollaroan sprang up from behind Kirkpatrick's desk.

"But Wentworth phoned us you were probably dead!" he gasped.

"Sorry to disappoint you, Hollaroan," Kirkpatrick said harshly. "What have you been up to?"

It took Hollaroan several moments to regain control, then he stammered out news in a swift stream . . . Tavish dead under the *Spider's* seal; Wentworth's warning that the Flame Master planned to loot the city; a report from the patrolman on the beat concerning the beer parlor to which Doña Margherita had phoned ....

"He says it's a Spanish hang-out," Hollaroan said rapidly, "and there's gossip about secret rooms connected with the building. Oh, yes, and the Spanish Consulate burned down with a loss of ten or twelve lives!"

Kirkpatrick came to his feet. "The consulate! Were the women saved?"

Hollaroan stepped back. "No one was saved, sir. I underhand Miss van Sloan was in the building at the time."

Kirkpatrick sank into his chair and, though Hollaroan kept talking, he heard the deputy only as an irritating noise.

"Get out!" Kirkpatrick ordered abruptly. "Call in all reserves and post them over the Manhattan area, especially below Canal Street. They're to await specific orders from me. If any radio car spots Wentworth, he's to be asked to call me. Now, get out. I've work to do!"

Hollaroan's face was flushed angrily as he strode from the office, but Kirkpatrick scarcely noticed him. Nita . . . dead! Wentworth would be a madman! No question as to what he would do. Dick would smash headlong into the ranks of the Flame Master and kill until he himself was slain! Kirkpatrick wavered for a moment over a thought that perhaps it were better so. Only Kirkpatrick, who knew them so well, realized how deep was his love for Nita. The shock might actually break the balance of Wentworth's finely attuned mind!

Kirkpatrick felt that his brain was extraordinarily clear, despite the furious activity of recent hours. Probably the effect of too much oxygen. Why, he even imagined he could smell ozone here in his office! Kirkpatrick laughed in self-mockery. To work now . . . He couldn't grasp the meaning behind Wentworth's warning: Tavish was dead and the Flame Master was going to loot the city. It didn't make sense. Certainly not! Kirkpatrick laughed again. He flung himself into a frenzy of work, posting reserves and emergency wagons over the downtown area, laying a trap that not even the Flame Master could break through ... he hoped!

For a half hour, he worked furiously and all headquarters whirled to the mad tune he played. Men laughed as they ran about errands, a new elation crept into the radio announcer's voice.

Sergeant Reams stood waiting for orders in the anteroom, with a party of raiders he had been ordered to assemble. He grinned at a companion.

"It's just like a pint of whiskey, having him back," Reams said.

The other man moved uneasily. "I don't like it. Weren't you telling me this ozone or something made people drunk?" He drew out a pack of cigarettes and tucked one between his lips, fumbled for a match.

Reams' grin blanked out for a moment, then he laughed. "If it was anything like that, the boss would know it. But I do feel a little queer."

The man had his match poised against the board, his eyes hard on Reams'. From inside the office, Kirkpatrick's laughter boomed.

"Here he comes," Reams hissed.

"Chuck that cigarette!"

The man obeyed just as Kirkpatrick came striding energetically from his inner office, his face flushed.

"We have a tip that looks like it might take us to the Flame Master's head-quarters," he said buoyantly. "Follow my car. Reams, with me!"

He reeled off balance a little, as he whirled, dragged a palm hard across his forehead. More fatigued than he realized, Kirkpatrick told himself, but he had to beat Wentworth to the saloon where, he was convinced, the Master had head-quarters. Kirkpatrick stopped and sniffed the air. Hell! That damned ozone must be in his very lung tissues!

"Hurry!" he flung at Reams and sprang into his car.

AS Kirkpatrick's car pulled out from the curb, Wentworth was racing to headquarters in a taxi. He sat bolt upright in the rear of the cab and his face, cut deep by haggard lines, was totally without expression. He seemed scarcely alive, save for the burning rage in his eyes.

Behind those burning eyes. Wentworth's brain clicked relentlessly on. There was a corner in his brain where horror lurked, a horror that threatened to blot out very sanity, but Wentworth penned it there. He could not think of *that*. He could not allow himself to think of that. Not until . . . His hands crept to the guns beneath his arms and expression crept into his face, twisted his mouth. The cab driver glanced over his shoulder, screamed. He grabbed for the brakes, leaped from the car and ran.

With a rasping curse, Wentworth sprang to the pavement. There was a gun in hand. It was in line before he checked himself. He looked at the gun and his hand began to tremble. The tremor raced over his body. God! Was he going mad! He pushed the gun, still with a palsied hand, clicking back into his holster, got behind the taxi wheel himself.

But it was a full minute before he could send the car forward. Slowly, the speed mounted. Wentworth stared almost blindly before him, steering like an automaton. The motor roared and the tires skidded wildly on icy turns, but he paid them no heed. He had to get to headquarters.

Remorseless logic had shown him what the Flame Master would do. No daring was beyond this man who planned to loot the city. Therefore, the police brain would be destroyed by bim; therefore he would burn headquarters and destroy radio and telephone coördination. Once that was done, the city would be at his mercy for hours .... If he had telephoned that, the fool deputy would have laughed at him. Kirkpatrick would have known better, but Kirkpatrick... Wentworth closed off his thoughts again. His face contorted, his mouth awry.

Wentworth became abruptly aware of dazzling light, of a blast that snubbed the taxi almost to a halt. His dazed eyes lifted and saw flame sheeting across the night sky. Too late! He was too late. Headquarters already had gone up in fire and smoke. Already, his hands were in motion, wrenching the taxi about, scooting back the way he had come. Well, the taxi driver wouldn't be able to report its theft now. No one would be able to report a theft of any kind. The Flame Master . . . had the city at his mercy!

The taxi was leaping and skittering over the snow-iced streets. Snow had stopped, and cold had touched the slush and made it solid. The cab careened wildly, but Wentworth's hands held it in control subconsciously, calculated the skids and utilized them. He ignored traffic lights, kept the horn down steadily as he hammered—hammered his way north. He had had a proposal to make to Deputy Hollaroan, that the police commandeer a radio station, have telephone calls transferred. Police authority would have made that easy, but without it . . .

His thoughts flashed to his Daimler. He had left it back there near the consulate, forgotten because of . . . of *that*. He'd have to go back there now. Wentworth's hands gripped the steering wheel so tautly that the ache crept up to his shoulders, but he scarcely heeded it. He forced himself to drive back to where the smoldering heat of the burned consulate still beat out into the night.

He kept his eyes turned from it, and the tears slid down his harsh-lined cheeks again. He flung himself behind the wheel of the Daimler, whirled and drove like mad away from that spot. Presently, he stopped and, in the curtained rear, opened the hidden wardrobe, the make-up table.

HIS eyes blurred under the strong lights, but he ignored the fact, began to smear make-up on his face. He made no effort to smooth out the lines, but emphasized the gauntness of his cheeks, altered the line of his nose and chin, rapidly fashioned a military mustache such as Kirkpatrick wore. His eyes were not the same frosty blue as Kirkpatrick's, but if his stride and voice tones were right, it would be improbable anyone would be suspicious.

He slid a Chesterfield coat from the rack, a derby hat and, on the way uptown, again forced himself to stop and purchase a gardenia which he pinned to his lapel. It might have been Kirkpatrick himself who went striding through the corridors of the broadcasting studios of the Amalgamated chain.

"Who's the highest official here tonight?" he rasped at an information clerk. "I'm Commissioner Kirkpatrick!"

The man got busy on the telephone. "Vice-President Carleton, sir," he reported. "Eleventh floor."

Without a word, Wentworth swung on his heel and it was with Kirkpatrick's choppy, military stride that he entered the elevator.

On the eleventh floor, he went striding straight to the vice-president's office, where a dozen people were waiting. The secretary looked up, startled, as Wentworth swept by her to the door of the private office. She sprang to her feet, but Wentworth was already inside.

"Mr. Carleton," Wentworth said in the clipped, rapid tones of Kirkpatrick. "I'm Commissioner Kirkpatrick, of the police. I have to see you at once on emergency business."

Carleton sprang to his feet, "Of course, Commissioner. I recognized you at once. Please excuse me . . ." He hurried two men out of the office. "Now, sir, I'm at your service!"

Wentworth nodded his thanks. "The criminals who are using fire as a weapon have destroyed police headquarters," he said curtly. "That means our radio is out of service, our telephones destroyed. It is the plan of the criminals to loot the city. I'll have to commandeer your radio station and switchboard."

Carleton's face was stretched into lines of amazement, of incredulity. "I can hardly believe..." he began. He stopped.

"I don't ask you to believe!" Wentworth's voice hardened. "Act! Get on that phone and have your power station change the wave-length to the official wave-band of the police. Get me a microphone in here connected with it. Find me a half-dozen intelligent persons to get on the telephones out there in the office. Your operators will relay all police calls there. I'll get hold of the telephone company, and make the arrangements. Move, man, the fate of thousands of human beings is in the balance!"

Driven by Wentworth's sharp urgency, Carleton staggered to the telephone and, as he spoke, his voice cleared, his energies revived. His voice began to crackle, too. Wentworth sprang to another telephone and shot through a call to the telephone company, got hold of their highest official on duty.

"Commissioner Kirkpatrick speaking," he rasped. "You know by now that police headquarters lines are down. Relay all calls to this exchange. Amalgamated radio. Get it working at once!"

He slammed up the telephone receiver and charged back into Carleton's office, and men ran in behind him with a microphone, already attached.

Carleton was still talking over telephones, giving orders to the switchboard, getting men and women at the telephones in the outer office. He hung up, staggered from the chair, and Wentworth dropped into it.

"Have those people in the outer office make intelligible notes on all calls and bring them to me here," he ordered. "If they have to talk to me personally, have calls switched to this phone." He moved the microphone and his hand was rock-steady. The phone jangled and Carleton grabbed it, smiled as he set it down.

"All right, Commissioner, you're on the air on your own wave-length, the moment you press that button on the mike."

Wentworth smiled dourly, "Thank you, Mr. Carleton. This won't be forgotten."

The phone bell jangled, and an excited voice demanded, "Police? This is the watchman at the Federal Reserve Bank. Listen, that fire smell I've been reading about in the newspapers is all over this building, and . . ." His voice broke in a scream and over the wire came the roar and crackle of an explosion, instantly cut off as the phone went dead.

Wentworth's hand flashed to the microphone. "Calling all cars," his voice rasped. "Commiss-ioner Kirkpatrick speaking. Ignore all previous orders. The Flame Men are attacking the Federal Reserve bank. All cars between Canal and Fulton streets: blockade all streets from the East River to the Hudson leading out of the financial district. Commandeer trucks and blockade the streets.

"Calling all cars between Houston and Canal Streets. You men will drive your cars to the barricade and mount it with machine guns. Firemen will be sent to you with asbestos suits.

"Calling all cars between Fulton Street and the Battery. Converge on area around the Federal Reserve Bank. Report by telephone at first opportunity. That is all."

Wentworth was laboring under a heavy handicap. He did not know the numbers of cars in the district, could only give blanket orders by area. He snatched a telephone and called Chief Donavan of the fire department, outlined the situation and ordered firemen to reinforce the barricades with hose and asbestos suits.

He snapped back to the microphone, "Sergeant Reams! Sergeant Reams, re-port to headquarters. That is all."

That was Kirkpatrick's private call. Wentworth had no thought that he might reach Kirkpatrick. He was sure his friend was dead, but if he could locate Reams he might gain more detailed information about the radio cars. Wentworth was being deluged with telephone calls from police, from other banks within the financial area. The Flame Men were striking in a dozen places at once. Carleton had brought a large map of the city. Wentworth rapidly diagrammed his strategies.

It was mad, frantic work, mostly blind. He knew a great deal about the police organization, due to his close friendship with Kirkpatrick, but he was laboring under an incredible handicap. His face was grim, eyes blazing as he snapped orders in response to phone reports. There had been no attempt yet to crash the barricade. Reserves were racing into the financial district, surrounding the blazing areas behind barricades of their own cars.

"Sergeant Reams!" Carleton called. "Sergeant Reams is here, Commissioner!"

Wentworth's eyes lifted as he barked orders into the microphone and saw a man in uniform enter the office, his stride brisk and military, close the door behind him. The man flung off his uniform cap, and Wentworth jerked to his feet.

"Kirkpatrick!" he gasped. *"Kirkpatrick!* Man, I thought you were dead!"

KIRKPATRICK'S taut lips stirred in a slight smile as he strode to the desk and their hands locked in a quick, hard grasp. Wentworth dropped back into the chair, moved the microphone forward and went on with the order, while his eyes held those of Kirkpatrick.

"You've probably saved the city, Dick," Kirkpatrick said quietly. "Why didn't you tell me you had already taken that saloon on the Bowery! I went there to save you."

He brushed words aside with a quick jerk of his hand, bent over the map. With staccato words, Wentworth explained what was being done. He slid out of the chair at the desk and gladly watched Kirkpatrick drop into it.

Wentworth's hands flew as he divested himself of his clothing. "No one must know you weren't here all the time."

Kirkpatrick nodded and unbuttoned the uniform while he took messages and shot his orders out.

Wentworth's eyes were burning again, and his face set in a relentless mold. Now, he could leave this desk-work and speed southward to the battle-front. He had no illusions about the police fight against the Flame Master. His body trembled with eagerness as he scrambled into the uniform and touched his holstered guns. Soon now, soon, he could avenge....

Kirkpatrick's back was toward him, studying the map as he pulled on clothing also. There was a momentary lull.

"Can't blame you for thinking me dead, Dick," he threw over his shoulder. "Would have been, too, but for an accident. When you worked out the way to attack those machine gunners, I rushed the one in the opposite direction by the same method. He ran and the mob poured out of the building. I was pushed along in front of it and before I could fight free, the building went up in flames... Dick, I lost forty-three men in that accursed Keystone Spire!"

Wentworth was wordless. He scarcely seemed to hear. He came back to Kirkpatrick and thrust out his hand.

Kirkpatrick straightened in surprise, "Stay here, Dick!" he cried. "I need your help!"

Wentworth's only answer was a savage grin. He pivoted and strode toward the door.

"Dick!" Kirkpatrick cried. "You can't bring her back by killing yourself! Stop, damn it, or I'll shoot . . ." He jerked out his long-barreled revolver.

Wentworth faced him in the doorway. He laughed and the sound of it was jarring and terrible. He flung back his head and laughed.

"Shoot and be damned to you!"

He opened the door and strode out. The door slammed hard behind him. Kirkpatrick stared down at the revolver, dropped into the chair. The telephone bell rang and he groped for it.

CHAPTER ELEVEN
Master of Hell

WENTWORTH'S race southward to the barricade was a continual careening challenge to death. A dozen times, he missed smashing his car to bits and himself with it, but he never eased his foot on the accelerator, scarcely glanced at the obstacles his skittering limousine grazed. At long last, he glimpsed the barricade ahead, trucks parked broadside across the streets. He heard the chatter of machine guns and the *whang* of riot guns; the blasts of grenades. It was warfare in the city streets.

Even as Wentworth charged for the barrier, crouched with locked hands upon wheel, a blast of flame rolled over the scene. In its midst, there was a thunderous blast and he saw the fragments of a heavy truck soar—black twisted steel against a sheet of red flame. The body of a man, scarcely recognizable, thudded to the pavement in Wentworth's path. He avoided it with a quick swing of the wheel, scarcely seeing it, eyes still focused on what was plainly a charge of the Flame Master's men through the barricade.

A chain of cars raced past the gaping depression in the earth where a bomb had blasted the truck. On the running-boards clung men in the flaming suits of the Horde, guns blasting in their hands. Wentworth laughed softly. He ground the accelerator to the floor and charged straight at the leading car! His lights were out and he was within a hundred feet of his goal before his charge was seen. A quick-sweeping volley of bullets met him, frosted over the bullet-proof windshield, clanged against the armored metal of the hood and frame.

He did not falter, did not swerve from his swift, sure course. A Flame Man leaped from the running-board of the first car and, slipping on the ice, skidded in a long head-first dive across the street. The driver attempted to dodge by a quick wrench of the wheel, and the car went into a slithering turn. It was broadside when the Juggernaut weight of Wentworth's heavy car rammed into its side.

It was a mad thing Wentworth had done and his survival was the result of fortunate circumstances rather than clear thought. The Daimler's weight and speed were twice that of the car it struck, and the icy pavement prevented the criminals' car from standing up to the shock. Its side was crushed in and it catapulted from the collision like a baseball. Wentworth was thrown heavily forward against the steering wheel by the impact. The Daimler faltered then charged on.

The smashed car met the second of the line of machines head-on, and the two reared into the air like fighting stallions. The third car tried to brake and went into a sliding, sideways skid toward the cavern the bomb had torn in the street. It teetered for a moment on the verge, toppled over as the Daimler flashed past into the street beyond the barricade. Behind Wentworth, guns were crashing once more.

Wentworth realized that the Daimler had trundled to a halt with a lamp post bent double over its steel top. He was dazed by concussion, reeling as he climbed from the car. His feet went out from under him, and he lay where he had fallen.

HE PEERED up at the sky, crimson with the glare of flames from a dozen fires. Men were running toward him, ducking from door to door. Bullets whined over his head. Slowly, Wentworth began to come out of his stupor. He saw men in crimson charging up the street, knew that guns from the barricade were answering them.

Wentworth braced both hands on the pavement and slid himself sideways until he lay against the side of the Daimler. He pulled out his automatics. Once more lead was hammering against the car, and Wentworth hegan to laugh softly. So, they

The first car was catapulted from the collision—

like a baseball driven by a champion's bat.

wanted to fight!

He pushed himself to his feet, braced a shoulder against the Daimler. He had an automatic in each fist and there were seven, no eight, of the Flame Men in sight. Two of them had machine guns, the rest hand-guns of some sort. Wentworth's lips drew back savagely from his teeth. He began to shoot, firing each gun alternately. His first two bullets dropped the machine gunners. He laughed and continued to fire, as deliberately as on a target range. And each time a man fell, his laughter lifted to the heavens. Flat, mocking, horrible—the laughter of the *Spider!*

Once he was driven back a half pace by lead that smacked into his body. He bent forward a little and kept on firing. Nine shots—and the eight Flame Men were down. Wentworth looked down at his body, saw a bloody tear across his right side. They'd have to shoot better than that to stop the *Spider* tonight! He was stuffing cartridges into his gun clips again, heard men's cheers behind him, the swift pound of running feet.

Wentworth whipped about. "Get back to that barricade, fool!" he shouted. "Hold the barricade and let me handle this!"

He opened the Daimler and knelt inside while he ripped off the tunic and dabbed his side with iodine from a compartment in the rear, plastered an adhesive pad across it. Not important, the wound, but he must keep this blood of his for a while. There was still the Master ....

When Wentworth went steadily down the street, he was in his shirt sleeves. He walked deliberately to the various bodies of the Flame Men until he found one about his own size, then dragged the body into a dark doorway.

Presently, from that doorway emerged another Flame Man with a machine gun. He turned his back on the police lines and ran frantically back toward the center of the fires, and he staggered as he ran. Other Flame Men began to shout at him presently but he did not answer them, pounded on, though under the hood hate twisted the face of Richard Wentworth! His hands twitched on the trigger of the machine gun in his arms.

At last, he found what he sought, another motorcar into which the loot of a bank was being loaded. He ran to the man who was bossing the operation.

"I have to reach the Master at once," he gasped, in Spanish. "The police have another radio station. I know where it is! Take me to the Master!"

Through the slits of the hood, his eyes were watching the man narrowly. It might be that he was supposed to know where the Master was. If this were so, he had betrayed himself. But he gambled on the secretiveness with which criminal masters guard themselves, and he was right.

The man whirled toward him. "Where is it?" he demanded. "Tell me quickly!"

"So you can claim the credit for it, thou dog!" Wentworth snarled. "Take me to him, I say!"

The man cursed and made a threatening gesture toward the holstered gun at his side. The muzzle of Wentworth's machine gun swung up. "That would be foolish," Wentworth said. "Shall I tell the Master that you kept me from him with an important message!"

"I'll go with you!" the man said. He whirled and snapped out an order to some one else to superintend the loading, ran toward a police roadster nearby. Wentworth saw the men, who had occupied it, dead upon the icy pavement and once more hatred flared up within him. He held it down, savagely. Only one thing was important now—to find and slay the Master!

THE other hooded man sprang to the wheel of the car, kicked the cold motor to life and whirled it in a tight U-turn, sent it hammering southward. Wentworth kept his eyes and his gun on the man, but out of the corner of his vision he could gauge their course—into Broadway and southward, past Trinity Church, past Bowling Green and out over the walkways of the Battery.

Wentworth strangled the hard laughter that rose in his throat. Of course, there would be another way of escape than through the barricade uptown. A boat—a swift boat that would open up to them all the avenues of New Jersey, and Long Island, of the Upper Hudson, for escape.

The car jerked to a halt and the hooded man sprang to the ground. Wentworth struck him across the head with the machine gun and slid his body under the car. There would be no need to waste bullets on *him*. He ran down the ramp of the covered dock and saw a yacht laid close against the wharf. No question of its power. It was Humboldt Tavish's Diesel-powered eighty-footer, and it could tear through the water at close to forty knots! Wentworth scrambled to the deck, and two men pointed guns at him.

"Drop that machine gun," one rasped. "You know better than to come aboard armed!"

Wentworth dropped the gun. "I have important information for the Master!" he cried. "The police have a new radio station, and I know where it is!"

The men motioned him down into the cabin, and Wentworth sprang for the door, threw it wide—and he was staring into the eyes of a man hooded like himself, garbed like himself. The Master?

"Speak fool!" the man ordered. "What is your message of importance?"

Wentworth eyed him closely. His au-

NEXT MONTH!

Satan's Switchboard

NEW YORK had known racketeers and murderous crime kings, but America's greatest metropolis was powerless in the steely grip of a nameless emperor of evil known only as — the Silencer! For the Silencer stopped at nothing, plundering the marts of trade; gutting the wealth of the city's banks; spreading a wave of frightful, inexplicable suicides; ensnaring the elite four-hundred in the tendrils of blackmail and kidnaping—and leaving in his wake the horribly branded bodies of those who had gained the slightest clue!

Only one man—Richard Wentworth—realized that the Silencer struck through the city's very pulse—its vast communications system! And Wentworth, in the weird garb of THE SPIDER, was the only man who had the stark courage and the resourcefulness to oppose the dreaded Silencer.

Don't miss the complete novel of a brave man fighting the most overwhelming odds!

THE MASTER OF MEN!

SPIDER

The December Issue! Out Nov. 5th!

This is the original advertisement from the November 1937 issue—
See page 112 for a preview of the next SPIDER thriller!

tomatics were beneath his scarlet uniform. This man's weapon was at his hip in an open holster. But was this the Master?

"Are you . . . the Master?" he asked hesitantly.

The man nodded curtly. "I have commanded you to speak!"

"Forgive me," Wentworth stammered. "I ... I did not know. The police have a new radio station. It is . . . ." He staggered and clutched his side, bent far forward. "Forgive me," he panted. "I am wounded." Frantically, his fingers fumbled at the fastenings of his uniform, reaching for a gun.

"Dog!" the man snarled.

His gun blasted, and Wentworth felt the lead course down his back, was driven to his knees. But he had his gun now. Twice, he squeezed the trigger and hammered lead up into that hooded face. The man was driven backward against the wall. He slammed to the floor.

The door behind Wentworth was wrenching open. He twisted that way and saw the two guards. One gripped the machine gun. Wentworth fired from the hip, but one of the men got off one shot. Wentworth felt his thigh driven back from under him and at that moment, somewhere aboard the ship, a woman screamed. At that scream Wentworth felt a shout rise in his throat!

He got to his one good foot and seized a chair as a brace. And, gun in hand, he moved toward the forward deckhouse.

And then Wentworth heard the woman's voice again. "Dick! Dick!" it cried. "Hurry, in heaven's ...."

WENTWORTH needed no more. The shout rose in his throat again and it was a shout of joy, of triumph. Nita! It was Nita who had cried to him. She was beyond that door. He must reach her.

Wentworth's gun bucked twice in his hand as he lunged forward. The bullets smashed the lock. He sprang through the doorway. Nita lay on the floor, blood on her temple. Doña Margherita was sprawled across a chair and, seated behind a desk, Don Carlos held a gun in his hand.

Those things, Wentworth saw in a flashing sweep of his eyes, but he saw more. Don Carlos was dead, and... The gun leaped from Wentworth's hand, hit by a bullet. Wentworth staggered under the impact, tried to catch himself and pitched to the floor. Through the forward doorway a hooded man in scarlet strode, long-barreled automatic in his hand.

The man laughed. "When your beloved recovers consciousness presently, she will find you dead and Don Carlos dead where I was sitting, with my hood upon him. They will be very sure that Don Carlos was the Flame Master, don't you think so, Wentworth?"

Wentworth rolled his head on the floor. "Not at all, Lebland," he said weakly. "They know who you are, though they didn't learn it until too late to catch you before this attack tonight."

The Master snarled, strode forward and drove his foot into Wentworth's side. "You lie, dog!"

Wentworth rolled with the kick. There was still a gun beneath his scarlet garb, if he could reach it. But he was very weak, bleeding from three wounds.

"What does it matter if I lie now?" he gasped. "I who am about to die! I tell you they know, Lebland!"

He twisted his head about painfully, as if he were too weak to move his body. Under him, his left hand crept toward the gun. "Shall I tell you how they know, Lebland?"

Lebland leveled the revolver at Wentworth's head, but waited, his eyes glinting through the slits of the hood.

"They know because you were too clever, Lebland," Wentworth panted on. "You were all set to let Tavish take the full responsibility. He was guilty—of hiring you. But his machinations were all financial. That was too slow for you. You wanted to loot, loot, loot! You feared Tavish would betray you, so you were set to throw the blame on him—and then we got Beulah Loraine before you were ready. You knew she would talk and that we would go after Tavish. You thought he would betray you, then. He did. He was already frightened and, before you could get there and kill Tavish, he phoned the story to .... some one. After that, you were going to use Don Carlos as a blind. You had kidnaped him for Tavish, because Tavish feared he might grow suspicious. So you see, Lebland, even if you escape from here, you will be caught, and you will die!"

Lebland was bending over him. "Not at all, Wentworth," he said. "I knew that Tavish phoned, but I thought it was to Margherita here. She admitted it was, but she probably lied, hoping I would be trapped. That was why I took her prisoner—to find out the truth. But they won't catch me, Wentworth. They won't catch me, because . . . *you are going to tell me to whom Tavish phoned!*"

Wentworth laughed weakly and Lebland kicked him again. It was what Wentworth wanted. It gave him a chance to double over, to get his fingers on the butt of the automatic. He writhed—and fired straight up into Lebland's face!

Lebland straightened under the blow of the lead, reeled backward, and Wentworth rolled and slowly, deliberately pumped every bullet in his automatic into that falling body. Slowly, then, he pushed himself to his feet. It was easy now. There was a radio on the ship and it would tell the police that the Master was dead. Once the Flame Men knew that, they would fall easy prey to the police.

Yes, it was all easy now. His wounds did not even pain. Nita . . . Wentworth dragged his wounded leg to her side and touched her hair gently, gently with the hand that had killed a dozen men this night. For a moment, he was there beside her, then he crawled away toward the radio cabin.

THE END

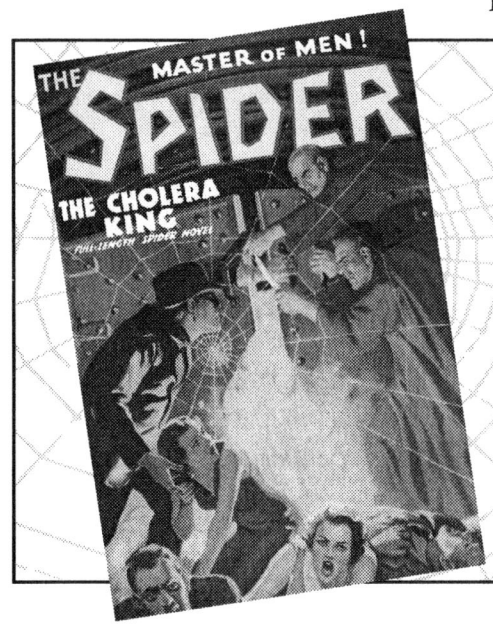

Doc Turner and the Crimson Coffin

A DOC TURNER STORY
By ARTHUR LEO ZAGAT

*The corpse pointed accusingly at
the man who had killed it!*

*Into Doc Turner's
little settlement drove
that terrible hearse with its death-trap
for the poor—a flaming crimson coffin. Only
the little druggist could beat this ruthless racket—
by making a corpse rise, of its own volition, from the grave!*

ORRIS Street, roofed by the seried black ties of the el, walled by dingy tenement fronts, floored by debris-strewn cobbles, was a long tunnel of drabness. Even the scarlet of radishes and tomatoes heaped on the pushcarts that lined its curbs, the emerald of lettuce and cabbage-heads, the brownspotted yellow of bananas,

served only to high-light the dim and brooding street.

A grey and feeble figure, Andrew Turner stood in the doorway of his drugstore and watched from beneath bushy white brows the shifting panorama of the slum.

Deepening dusk, elsewhere melancholy enough, seemed here a slow settling of doom. The old druggist felt in his bones the vague unease, an evasive sense that something was deadly wrong. The seams of age etched his face more deeply, so that its kindliness was bleakly masked.

There beat about Doc the brawling tumult which he had become accustomed through long years—the harsh shouts of the hucksters, the pounding rush of traffic, the shrill screams of halfclad, grimy youngsters at play in the hazardous gutter, the polyglot chatter of their alien elders for whom a golden promise had faded into the reality of poverty and unremitting toil. To the nostrils of his great, bony nose came the compound odor of garbage and sweat of unwashed bodies, and breath odorous with exotic foods. Everything was as it always was, yet deep in Doc Turner's bleared, blue eyes crawled a secret anxiety, and they were keenly watchful.

He was the only friend of those who were bewildered strangers in a strange land. He was their adviser, their interpreter of customs they did not understand. And he was more.

Among those who live without the law there are those who batten only upon the very poor because they are ignorant and helpless. Human rodents are these, without courage but shrewd and ruthless and, if cornered, more vicious than their braver fellows. Against them, Andrew Turner protected his people. Against them, he waged an unremitting war and, as to every hunter, whether of beasts or of men, there had come to him an inexplicable instinct for their evil presence, an awareness of their depredations depending upon no concrete evidence but as sure as if he watched them at their nefarious work.

This instinct was warning him now. Something was wrong on Morris Street.

There was work for him to do.

But what?

NO USE, he knew, to ask of this bearded Hebrew, that swarthy son of Sicily, why their glances shot with covert fearfulness through the shambling sidewalk throng—why, beneath their dark skins' stolidity, there was a faint pallor of apprehension, a quiver of dread. Much as they respected him, much as they loved him, they would not reply. Schooled to silence by generations of persecutions and banditry, they would look at him blandly, a veil dropping over their eyes, shrug expressive shoulders and turn away.

He must wait till something happened .... Unaccustomed sounds interrupted the aged pharmacist's thoughts; the clop-clop of hoofs on the cobbles, the jingle and slap of harness and rumble of iron-tired wheels.

Even before Doc turned, he knew that for which he was waiting had come. A hush had traveled toward him with the sound of the horses, heads turning out there along the street, a sigh that ran along beneath the el like a wind through elms that had not been here for two decades. Then he saw the horses and what they drew, and a pulse thudded in his temples.

There were two of them, deep-chested, great-hewed draft animals sleekly black, squat but so huge-bodied as to seem monstrous.

They plodded slowly toward him between the gaunt pillars of the el and about their deliberate progress there was a grim, relentless quality inevitable as the coming of night.

They drew a sideless truck painted a lustrous black to match their hides. Blotched against a wavering luminescence, its driver was a hunched black bulk without form or face, erect and swaying with the swaying of the truck.

This strange equipage came opposite Doc Turner. He saw now that the light moving with it came from smoking flames that topped four tall, arm-thick candles set at the corners of the vehicle's flat bed. And he saw the truck's unbelievable load. It was merely a coffin, but it was crimson as spurting arterial blood, crimson as the petals of an opium-bearing poppy struck through by the sun.

Because the illumination by which it was startlingly visible was unsteady, the casket's blasphemous color throbbed with constant change, so that its substance seemed in some macabre manner alive. What that substance was the old druggist could not at once make out, but it was not quite opaque, and within it was discernible the vague shadow of a corpse.

On the sidewalk no one made a sound after that first sigh, and no one stirred. The only noise in the hush was the clop-clop of those horses' hoofs and the slap-jingle of their harness. The only movement in the trailing dusk was the movement of the truck.

AND then abruptly there was new sound and new movement. An over-alled young Slav, thick-necked, thick-limbed, thrust between two carts into the gutter. His face was pallid with wrath, his fisted arm rising above his head. From five yards away his voice, guttural but shrill-edged, shouted at the truck.

"Damn you!" it shocked the silence. "Damn you! You no scare me wid your tricks! You no get . . ."

He pitched forward, thudded on the cobbles, twitched and was very still.

For an instant more, the crowd on the sidewalk was immovable, not yet comprehending what had occurred. The grotesque hearse turned the corner into Hogbund Lane, plodding measuredly.

Doc sprang into motion toward that corner, was blocked by rigid bodies. Between heads and shoulders, he saw the gaping face and blue uniform of a policeman.

"Stop that truck, Casey!" he yelled. "Hold it!"

The patrolman swung to obey. Street lamps flared on, obliterating the dusk with garishness, and a woman screamed.

That shrillness was like a knife edge. It released a welling, chaotic tumult of shouts, and Morris Street was abruptly a blundering, milling mass.

The little pharmacist thrust between a whimpering Swede and a shawled Polish woman from whose hand a market bag had spilled. He got through the jostle, over the curb, and went to his knees in the gutter alongside the man who had dropped there in the middle of that defiant shout.

The powerful frame was limp and its head lolled laxly sidewise on the smeared stone. Glazed eyes stared at Doc—sightless eyes. He knew that they would never see again, yet he reached for the flaccid wrist, his acid-stained, gnarled fingers finding the place where a pulse should be. There was, of course, none there.

But there was no visible wound—no injury of any kind to explain that sudden death. Under the corner of the man's jaw there showed simply a little patch of reddened skin where the rough collar of his tieless shirt might have rubbed.

"Ivan!" a feminine voice wailed over Doc's head. "Ivan!"

The woman dropped beside Doc, her flaxen hair disordered, her high-cheek-boned, broadly sculptured face distorted almost beyond human semblance. "I know you get mad too quick sometime ..." A sob choked her, visibly wrenching her larynx. Her toil-roughened hands clawed the lifeless head to her lap, and she rocked above it, moaning.

"Steady, Mariovna," Doc said gently. "You have your two little ones."

Realizing the futility of proffered comfort at the moment, he pushed erect, shoving through the knot now closing a tight circle on the tragedy. He reached the sidewalk and corner.

THE policeman at whom he had shouted was coming toward him... and the black truck with its burden was nowhere in sight. "Casey!" Turner exclaimed, grasping the cop's sleeve. "Where is it? You let it get away!"

"Sure, Doc, and how was I goin' to hold him? He had a permit for displayin' an advertising float in the precinct and he didn't violate no ord'nance. If he had any pull at all it would of been my badge if I made him stop."

"Violate an ordinance!" the druggist exclaimed. "Would any pull take your badge away for arresting a murderer? Didn't you see Ivan Petroff drop dead as he shouted at him?"

"Sure Doc," Casey returned. "Sure I seen the hunkie drop. But he wasn't within fifteen feet of the truck, and the guy on it didn't make no move. Petroff just got excited and his heart conked. Many times them big bums is like that— look like bulls but all rotten inside. The guy in black didn't have nothing to do with it. If he's a killer, I snatched Judge Crater."

The pharmacist's lips pressed thinly together beneath his nicotine-browned mustache. The damage was done and discussion with this bovine representative of the law was utterly futile.

"You're right," he said, his tone colorless. "The man on the truck could have had nothing to do with it. Which way did he go?"

"Down there," Casey's ham-like paw gestured to the slope of Hogbund Lane, a tenement-sided gut sloping toward the river. "He whipped up his horses after he showed me his permit and he turned north again on Pleasant Avenue."

"Who is he? What did he look like?" the Doc snapped.

The officer shrugged. "I dunno. He didn't take his mask off. He didn't even say nothing but just shoved his paper at me, holding it in a black glove."

"There must have been a name on the permit."

"Sure. The Sun Trucking Company.

They kind of make a specialty of these here floats, and the permits are always made out to them. Say listen, Doc, I can't stand palavering here with you no longer. I got to take care of that stiff."

"Yes," Turner sighed. "Yes. You have to take care of Ivan. You have to have the carrion taken away because it's blocking traffic."

Casey didn't hear him, probably would not have understood had he heard. Casey was going to the police phone box fastened to the sidewall of Doc Turner's drugstore. Time enough to take a look at the stiff after he called in his report.

If he had troubled to go right to the dead man he would have seen something that was holding the watching crowd numb in a sickened sort of awe. The red spot on Petroff's neck was spreading. It was the breadth of one's hand now, and it was crimson as the petals of a poppy through which the sun struck.

Before the medical examiner ordered the body taken to the morgue for an autopsy that scarlet had spread till the whole cadaver was the color of spurting, arterial blood.

FOUR hours later, Morris Street was just as it had been—or almost so. There was a note in the raucous cries of the peddlers that had not been there before. There were no yelling children playing in the gutter, and miraculously escaping destruction under the Juggernaut wheels of traffic. And, though the street lamps, store windows and the globes suspended over the pushcarts made the night garish, a dark river of some secret fear ran under the black roof of the el.

Within Andrew Turner's ancient drugstore, a barrel-chested squat young man with hair exactly the color of a freshpulled carrot, shrugged burly shoulders. The smile on his blunt-jawed face was rueful.

"The fellow at the Sun Company don't know who it was hired the truck from him," he said. "Whoever it was paid cash for it, and left a deposit. He didn't even come back with it but got off somewhere around the corner and let the horses go to the stable alone. The coffin wasn't on it any more."

Jack Ransom was a mechanic working in a garage around the corner from the pharmacy. He was Turner's right hand in his forays against the crooks who prey on the helpless poor, his fists the old man's bludgeon.

"I didn't think we'd find out anything that way." Doc probed the edge of a dingy-white showcase with a gnarled thumb. "But we had to try."

"You were calling the medical examiner's office when I came in. What did the autopsy show?"

"Death by apoplexy. Petroff's blood was charged with a tremendous amount of suprarenalin, the ductless gland excretion that pours into it with anger. So much that it kept on contracting the capillaries even after he was dead, the blood in them bursting them. That's why he turned red."

Ransom winced at the picture evoked by the old man's words. "That settles it, then," he said. "You don't want to find the driver of that truck any more. Petroff died by natural causes."

Doc's eyes narrowed. "No," he said softly. "It doesn't settle anything. Petroff was murdered ...."

"Good Lord, Doc!"

"And there will be others murdered around here, son, if they defy whatever it is of which that crimson coffin is the symbol. The police are through, Jack. That means it's once more up to us. We've got to stop it."

"To stop what? What's going on?"

"I don't know," the old man whispered. "I don't know. But it's something big. That show wasn't put on to goad one almost penniless laborer to his death. It was deliberately devised to strike terror into the people around here, to batter down their resistance to—" He broke off.

"To what?"

"I don't know, but —"

He broke off again. This time, however, it was because the drugstore door was opening.

THE wizened man who came in was cloaked in a dirty linen smock, and his crescent beard of black crinkled hair, his mustached thick lips, the humped promontory of his nose, left no question as to his race. He had a crumpled paper in one hand.

"Hello, Izzy," Ransom greeted him. "How's the *schochet* business? Slicing a lot of chickens' necks?"

Izzy's thin shoulders lifted to the level of his fanlike ears. "Ach," he whined. "Ees no beezness at all hardly. Dey ain't got eet no money to buy cheeckens around here no more. Dey got money hardly to buy zup meat."

"Huh. I thought you told me last week everything was on the up and up since the depression was over."

"Dot Vas lest week. Dees week—nodeengs. I kent understand eet." He turned to the druggist. "Dukter Toiner, mebbe you vill be so kindly to read me dees paper. A man geeve eet to me joost now und he said I moost be sure to read eet eef I know vot's goot fahr me."

The Doc took the sheet and read—

You cannot escape death. It may be tonight, it may not be for a long time. But when death comes to you, as come it must, you want to be prepared. You can be certain of a beautiful grave without having to pay out a lot of money now. A dollar a week is all we ask. As your friend, we advise you to come to 6197 Pleasant Avenue and make arrangements to start. Don't delay. Act now or—

"The corner of this paper is pasted over what follows the 'or'," Doc explained his break, picking at the glued flap.

"Ach," Izzy shrugged. "Ah plot in der Rodeph Sholem cemetery I got already yet. Vot do I need..." He stopped talking, and abruptly a grey film blurred the swarthiness of his visage. "Ai!" he wailed, his pupils dilating. "Aiaiai .... "

"Jack!" Doc Turner blurted. "Look here. Look at this."

There were no more printed words under the flap. There was only a blotch, slant-sided, the corners at one end cut off. A coffin—a scarlet colflu!

"Aiaiai," Izzy wailed. "Vot ees dot arttess ? Vot ees eet? I moost go..."

"Wait!" Doc's command was neither loud nor harsh, but some quality of command in it stifled the *schochet's* outcry. *"Wait!* I'll take care of this."

"Baht . . ."

"But nothing. You can't pay out a dollar a week the rest of your life. None of the people on Morris Street can. It's not only chicken they won't be able to buy,

it's the soup meat you mentioned."

"Baht eef we don't pay eet ve veel die like Petroff, ve veel die de red deat'."

"No. You will not die. None of you will die. Leave this to me. You know you can trust me."

"Thees ees deeferent."

"It is the same. Leave this to me, Izzy. Give me till tomorrow morning. Then, if I have not stopped this thing you can go ahead. Tell the others who got this circular the same."

"I dun't know no odders who got eet. Dere vas only me."

Turner did not seem to be surprised by this statement, although the live poultry market where the man worked was the center of slum gossip and if there had been more of the circutars he surely would have heard it.

"All right," the old druggist said. "Go home, stay there, and forget about this."

Izzy shambled out. "That's the stunt, is it?" Ransom growled. "The meanest racket of all, milking these poor guys for a grave in some lousy lot out in the sticks or maybe none at all. Buy a grave or else! Let's get the cops."

"No," Turner responded. "The police won't believe it. They have their verdict on Ivan's death and they'll say the truck was just a clever publicity stunt. It's still our job, Jack. It's still up to us."

"Let's get going then. It's ten o'clock now. And you told Izzy you'd settle this by morning."

A smile licked Doc Turner's lips, but there was no humor in his eyes. Only a bleak resolve.

"Make haste slowly, son," he said. "There are some things we have to do. first. For instance, you have to go up the block to Lapidus' Novelty Store and get me some stage hair, black and kinky, and some spirit gum. That's for a beard like

Izzy's. My nose is enough like his to pass muster, and I have some black hair dye for my eyebrows and mustache that will wash out easily. If I ever get a chance to wash it out."

THERE are degrees even in poverty and degradation. If Morris Street was a drab tunnel, Pleasant Avenue was a fetid, open sewer. The sparse street lamps here waged a futile struggle against a mucid darkness, and the cold-water flathouses seemed on the point of collapse. On the broken flagged sidewalks dough-faced humans shambled furtively about their shady business or loitered on railingless stoops or flaking curbs.

The Doc finally found Number 6197, hesitated, almost visibly took himself by the back of his greasy collar and forced himself up the worn steps of its stoop.

In the black maw of the vestibule a blacker figure materialized from the shadows. "Who yuh lookin for?" a palpably disguised voice demanded.

"I dun' know," the visitor whined. "De paper said come here und here I em."

"What paper?"

"De paper wit' de red coffin on eet. Maybe dees is not de place?"

"Yeah. It's the place. Go on in." Doc fumbled past the sentry. His groping hands found a door that swung open. He hesitated a moment, went through into sightless dark.

Unseen fingers closed on his elbow and he was conscious of a bulky presence beside him. The hand on his elbow shoved him silently forward. His own shoes made a sliding noise on bare wood beneath them but the feet of the other sounded only in a barely audible pad, as though it were some gigantic cat that guided him by an inexorable pressure.

He was turned at right angles, halted.

From just ahead of him there came a muffled rap, and then, though the stygian murk lessened not at all, he was aware that space had opened ahead of him. He was pushed into it, brought to a halt once more. Hinges whispered behind him and his straining ears caught the slither of a door into its frame.

"Veil," he said. "Vot ees dees?"

"Silence!" a hollowed voice intoned. Abruptly, there was light, four yellow pinpoints of light enclosing Doc in their square. They grew, became flames at the tops of arm-thick tall candles, and a room rose out of the darkness.

It was bare-walled, bare-floored. its two windows, straight ahead of Turner, were covered with black cloth tacked closely to their frames. Between them, between two of the candles, was the shapeless black figure of the horse-truck's driver. And on the floor right before the daring druggist was the crimson coffin the truck had carried.

HE COULD look down into the coffin because its cover was removed. He could see its interior, lined with red satin, and he could see the corpse whose presence had been before only shadowed through the casket's sides of translucent, scarlet glass. It was the clothed corpse of a man, and its skin was crimson as the puffed satin on which it lay.

"Why have you come here?" The hollow voice spoke again, and now it came from the monstrous, black-robed form.

"Fahr vy you esk? Deedn't de paper say I should come here?"

"The paper. Ah. Is this one of those we have summoned here?"

"Aye, Master Death." It was a voice from behind Doc that responded. "He is one of those." Doc threw a swift glance behind him, saw two men standing close to him. "He is on your list." They were not robed, but they wore black suits with collars turned up about their necks, black gloves and black masks through whose eye-slits was visible only a glitter.

"Are you ready to enter into an agreement for the purchase of a grave?" demanded Master Death.

"Vell," Doc shrugged in a perfect imitation of Izzy's gesture. "I dun't know. Mybe I dun't understand right vat you mean by vat you say on de paper, und de pickshoor of a red coffin. Suppose I dun't bny from you a grave."

"Then you will need one sooner than you think, Isadore Rifkin. Ivan Petroff thought that he did not need to deal with me and you saw what happened to him."

"De police doctor said eel vas—apoplexy. Dod deedn't have noddeng to do mit you."

"Petroff did not die of apoplexy, fool. He died because he defied me, and it was I who struck him down. Do you believe that or must I prove it to you?"

"Vy should I believe eet. I ...."

"Hell, chief," the man behind Doc exclaimed. "What's the idea of kidding around like this? We had rehearsals enough. Let this guy know we're on to him and get through with it."

"Vot you mean?" Doc exclaimed, starting to twist around. He never completed the movement. Steel-like hands blackgloved, grasped his shoulders and held him immovable. The second man reached out, ripped the false beard from his chin!

MASTER Death laughed, triumphantly and without humor. "They told us you were clever, Mister Andrew Turner," he said. "But you certainly did not show that tonight. There was only one circular sent out and that was intended to bring you here. It did just that."

Turner Seemed undisturbed. "Yes," he said. "It brought me here. But why did you bait this trap for me?"

"Because we heard all about you when we were looking the ground over before we started. It sounded like you were too good to be true, so we decided to let you ride but to keep an eye on you. When you sent your boy friend out to trace the truck, that was a warning that you were going to try to interfere with us and so... Well, here you are."

Doc sighed. "Here I am. What are you going to do with me?"

"Wouldn't you like to know?" the leader of the trio sneered.

"Yes. Not that it matters much. I am an old man and I'm living on borrowed time. But there is something that I'm really curious about."

"That is .... ?" Long experience with criminals had taught Turner that they shared one common failing, an overpowering inquisitiveness and an overweening propensity to boast of their cleverness. He was playing for time, and he took advantage of his knowledge now.

"I know why Petroff died," he said. "You shot a tremendous dose of adrenaline into his blood, of course, that the medical examiner's pathologist found and decided was suprarenaline—another name for the same compound—from the man's own gland. What puzzles me, however, is how you managed to do that. You were at least five yards away from him when he dropped."

Master Death chuckled. "That was simple. I had a sharp sliver of crystallized adrenaline in a blowpipe. He was near enough for it to penetrate his jugular when I expelled it. It could not be heard nor seen, and he died almost at once so he could say nothing of the sting he felt."

"Ingenious," Doc exclaimed. "Almighty ingenious. Too bad you are devoting that ingenuity to despoiling mankind instead of helping it."

"That is a slave morality to which I do not subscribe. I..."

"Hey, boss," the first interrupter growled again. "This yammering going to keep up all night? We got to take another trip around before the pushcarts is all off Morris Street. How about it?"

"All right, Luke. I'll get it over with. Turner, you're going to get a chance to gain first-hand knowledge of how it feels to die of an overdose of adrenaline." Master Death snapped, "Because . . ." There was movement in his black robes, and suddenly a thin rod projected from them, near their top, "Because you're going to die the way Petroff died."

"No!" Doc screamed. "No!" He tore free from the hands that held him, clapped a hand to his neck as though to shield it from the blowpipe missile.

Whiff the slender rod said, and Doc pitched forward over the scarlet coffin. He dangled there, motionless.

Master Death laughed again. "That's that," he granted. "He was too smart for his own good . . . but just smart enough for ours. We'll have a real corpse now to show any Doubting Thomases, instead of that wax dummy. Luke, you help me get it out of there and put Turner in. Dan, tell Steve to come in so the three of us can carry the casket out to that new wagon you have waiting in the back alley."

Dan went out. Between them the two others heaved Andrew Turner's still warm body from the coffin, lifted the stiff wax figure from the scarlet satin, replaced it with the corpse of the old druggist.

"It's going to give me a big kick," Luke chuckled as he slid the scarlet casket lid in place, "watching you drive along Morris Street with the stiff of this guy they're all crazy about."

"It will be a rather good joke," the other replied. There was a note of uneasiness in his tone. "Wonder what's keeping Dan and Steve."

"Probably sneaking a smoke before coming back," Luke proffered.

"Better go and see. I want to get started."

Master Death was alone in the candle-lit room. He fished in the stygian swirl of his macaber robes. His black-gloved hands came out with six wing-nutted silver screws. He bent to fit the first in the hole in the lid where it belonged—and froze!

The lid was lifting, slowly, apparently of its own volition! It rose bigher and higher... jumped upward and fell off.

Doc Turner heaved upright out of the casket—*the corpse of Doc Turner scarlet as blood save for black dyed mustache and eyebrows!* His scarlet hand jerked out, jabbed an accusing finger straight into the staring face of the man who had killed him!

"He whose name you stole calls for you," he rasped. "Come!"

THE black-robed man staggered backward, caught hindself. "Damn!" he grated, "for a minute you had me." There was a gun in his gloved hand, a nickeled automatic on which the flickering candlelight gleamed. "Missed you, did I? But I'll make sure of you this ...."

A sledgehammer fist pounded the weapon from his grip, and he was held helpless in throttling, whipcord arms—in the inexorable arms of a carrot-headed youth who grinned happily the while he said, "Gosh, Doc, you look like a Comanche on the warpath. How did you get that way?"

"Red ink, Jack," Andrew Turner auswered. "And I hope it's washable. Got enough rope left to tie him up?"

"Yeah. In the left pocket of my coat."

While the pharmacist fished out the thongs and busied himself lashing wrists and ankles of Master Death, he asked, "Did you get it all?"

"Sure Doc. I conked the lookout right after he passed you, and I listened to every word that was said in here. We certainly got enough on these birds to send them to the electric chair like they was on a greased slide. Then when Dan started out I stunned him before he knew what hit him, and the same for that bloke Luke. But what was the idea of jumping out of the box before I had a chance to get in?"

"I didn't quite fancy the idea of being screwed in there. Air was getting short, and I didn't know how long you'd be. Well, we can go back and tell Izzy he needn't worry any longer."

Jack stepped back from the trussed-up Master Death. "What I don't get is how you kept that dose of adren—adrenal—whatever it is that he shot into you from hurting you."

"That was simple. At the instant he blew the blowpipe I jabbed nayself with a hypodermic injection of nitroglycerine, which has exactly the opposite effect to the adrenaline. Either was a fatal dose, but the two neutralized one another and left my blood vessels normal. You see, Master Death," Andrew Turner allowed himself a moment of gloating, "my eyes were not too old to see that the circular you had handed to Izzy, knowing he would bring it to me to read, was not actually printed but drawn with india ink in a remarkably perfect imitation of printing. That warned me it was bait for a trap, and I came prepared. I was never in any real danger."

"No," Jack Ransom said dryly. "You was never in any danger. Not much!"

THE END

Death O'Clock Joy-Ride

Brother Henry hurled himself at Ackerman.

A BROTHER HENRY STORY
By
WAYNE ROGERS

Brother Henry had fought crime with brain as well as fists, but when his beloved young people were spirited away from the Five Corners Mission, he had his strangest battle—a fight to the finish with a Nemesis in a yellow car who chauffeured joy-riders to hell!

THERE was a troubled question in Brother Henry's eyes as he watched the last straggling member of the public-speaking classes leave the meetingroom of the Five Corners Community House. John Smith, his assistant, was already turning back the seats, gathering together a few scraps of littered paper, tidying up before the hall would be darkened—and, behind his inscrutable, square-jawed face, Brother Henry knew there existed the same disturbing thought.

Brother Henry's lips thinned.

The weekly sessions of this class had always been one of the most popular of the center's activities with the young people of the neighborhood. Lately, however, something had gone wrong. Attendance had been dropping off badly in the past few weeks, especially with the young men. Tonight at least a dozen, formerly regulars, had been absent. Young people whose sudden loss of interest was unaccountable—like Ben Reardon, captain of the class debating team. Ben had always been so enthusiastic, so vitally interested. So had Nancy Carey, his fiancée.

A wholesome, devoted couple—Brother Henry had watched the development of their romance with a benign, approving eye; and now that neither of them had been near the Community House for several weeks he felt their deflection keenly. He was aware of something more, too—that vague sixth sense that often warned him when things were not as they should be at the Five Corners....

In his years of devoted service to the heterogeneous assortment of peoples who constituted his strange flock, Brother Henry had learned that unexplained absentees of this sort usually spelled trouble. Often they were merely the surface indications of undercurrents swaying these unsuspecting souls, sweeping them toward destruction they were not sufficiently keen to perceive, themselves.

It was why he was still there in this section of the city which many others had long since deserted as a hopeless slum. It was why he had devoted more than twenty years to a leadership which ranged from the capacity of friend and adviser to that of two-fisted fighter and crooks' Nemesis—the champion of those who could not defend themselves:

"We're not able to give them evening clothes and cabaret entertainment," John Smith dryly put their mutual thoughts into words as he finished his tasks.

"That's the answer. You'll find them in the Golden Grotto any night—"

"But the Golden Grotto is expensive," Brother Henry's placid face was lined with worry as he envisioned the uptown tourist cabaret located at one end of the Five Corners. "It isn't a place for our people; doesn't even expect their patronage—"

"—any night they're not sitting around in the Nonpareil Social Club," John Smith finished as if he had not heard the interruption.

The Nonpareil Social Club—there was a thorn in Brother Henry's side! Every so often the young men of a community develop this club urge and rent a store to establish headquarters for their newly formed organization. He was accustomed to that—but this Nonpareil Club was different. It was no spontaneous development of the fraternal instinct; instead, it was the creation of an individual, Manny Ackerman, and ever since Manny Ackerman had come to the Five Corners—

The wail of police sirens out in the street seemed to echo the sudden disquiet in Brother Henry's heart; seemed to put into terrifying sound the very thought that was in his mind. Ever since Manny Ackerman had come to the Five Corners the wail of police sirens had become all too familiar!

THE speeding radio cars were already past the Community House when Brother Henry and Smith reached the door, but there was no difficulty trailing them. Those wailing sirens seemed to be converging from all sides— on a spot not more than two blocks from the building. It was Joe Caproni's grocery store.

Brother Henry identified their destination as he raced down the street already beginning to glut with anxious-eyed people calling to one another in a babel of languages to find out the meaning of this latest trouble tocsin. Joe Caproni's grocery store—and as he made his way through the gathering crowd, and stepped through the aromatic smelling doorway, he saw Caproni lying on the floor. The front of his white shirt and apron were stained with a widening pool of blood.

"Another hold-up," Sergeant O'Malley clipped as he recognized Brother Henry and stepped aside to let him kneel beside the stricken man. "We've sent for a doc, but it doesn't look like much use."

There wasn't any use. Brother Henry could see that much the moment he looked into Joe Caproni's face. The man's eyes already were glazing, his breath barely wheezing through blood-filling lungs. Joe Captoni was almost dead. Yet, in the last few moments of his life he recognized the friend of years now trying to ease his pain. Desperately, he clutched Brother Henry's arm, struggling to tell him something.

"Benny—Benny, he—" he managed, and then a red tide welled up in his throat and drowned his words in the gurgle of death.

Stony-eyed, Brother Henry stared down at the dead face as he lowered Joe Caproni to the floor. In that bitter moment, he recalled a hundred kindnesses the good-natured old Italian had shown to those less fortunate than he and who could not pay for the food he had to sell.

And now Joe Caproni was dead—murdered for the few miserable dollars his till would yield to the thief who had come in to rob him ....

Brother Henry started to arise from beside the body—when suddenly his whole being seemed turned to ice. His eyes, wide, staring things over which he had no control, were riveted on a tiny object lying on the floor near Caproni's head—the metal cap of a pocket pencil. It was from a pencil such as he had given each member of the public-speaking class for a present the past Christmas!

For a split-second he balanced there, a living statue, and then he seemed to lose his balance and topple over on the floor beside the corpse. But, when he got to his feet, his right hand was palming that damning cap, slipping it into his pocket until he would have the chance to scrutinize it—without surrendering it to the police.

Almost, he knew what he would find on that bit of yellow metal—yet when he peered down at it he felt his blood run cold in his veins. There on the cap, inscribed unmistakably, was the name *Ben Reardon!*

SICK at heart, Brother Henry stood, face to face with the realization that what he had secretly been fearing had actually taken place: a dozen of his best young men who had been corraled by this Nonpareil Social Club had been organized into a gang of thieves—and now of murderers!

During the past month there had been half a dozen hold-ups in the Five Corners, and defenseless proprietors of neighborhood stores robbed of their day's receipts. But this was the first time there had been a killing. Always the hold-ups had been a one-man job—a man masked and dressed so carefully that identification had been impossible.

But even though there was no way of proving his guilt, Brother Henry was morally certain that it could be laid at the door of Manny Ackerman. The planning was too clever, the execution too perfect for a beginner in crime. This neighborhood reign of terror bore all the earmarks of direction by a master hand—and Manny Ackerman was no tyro in the ways of the underworld.

Ackerman was twenty-six or seven; a man darkly, recklessly handsome in spite of the lines dissipation had already etched in his face. He was a native of the Five Corners, though he had left the neighborhood at an early age to take up his residence in a reform school. From that institution he had graduated to the ranks of petty gangdom. He had made some money—and now had come back to dazzle his old neighbors with flashy clothes and the expensive, canary-yellow automobile he kept stored in what was once a stable and blacksmith shop.

Those things Brother Henry knew about Manny Ackerman, but there were other things he suspected and feared. For one thing, he feared the effect of the swaggering gangster's self-importance on the youth of the Five Corners. A display of wealth such as Ackerman affected was dazzling in a section where a few penhies counted for so much.

That, Brother Henry was sure, was the secret of the Nonpareil Social Club's appeal—and now this recruiter for the ranks of the underworld had gotten his slimy tentacles around Ben Reardon ....

But a stop could be put to that. He would talk with Nancy Carey; see if she couldn't bring the boy to his senses. If only he could locate Ben there might still be some explanation for that damning pencil cap.

Hoping against hope, Brother Henry finally got away from the crowd around Caproni's store. Carefully, making sure that he was not being followed by suspicious police or lynx-eyed criminals, he made his way through the nearly empty streets until he reached the six-story tenement that was Nancy Carey's home. The block was dingy, deserted—the house, itself, a nondescript brick building that had long since lost all color; a bleak structure as run-down as most of its teeming denizens.

There was no light in the dirty, plaster-cracked vestibule, but the inner door was open, hooked back. Brother Henry could distinguish a young couple standing close together at the edge of a ring of light cast by a fitful gas-jet halfway down the long, bare hallway. Carefully, he slipped through the vestibule and to one side of the hall, to get a better view of the absorbed couple.

There was something familiar about the girl—and then he knew that he was right. She was Nancy Carey, standing there clasped in the arms of Manny Ackerman!

Brother Henry felt his blood boil as if it were his own sweetheart he saw there in the arms of another man. There was something so fine and sweet about Nancy that the thing he was watching seemed a sacrilege—made him want to get his fingers around the fellow's throat as Ackerman's lips closed over hers.

"Remember now," he heard the fellow husk throatily. "It's gonna be ten-thirty Saturday."

And Nancy Carey clung to him.

"I'll be there," she whispered as he started away from her—and then Brother Henry had to get out of that hallway in a hurry.

ALL, the way back to the Community House the events of the evening paraded through his mind while he tried to work out the pattern he felt sure they must make. The half-deserted public-speaking class, Caproni lying dying on the floor, Ben Reardon's pencil cap near the grocer's body, Nancy Carey in Manuy Ackerman's arms—somewhere they all tied up with the coming Saturday night.

"There is something evil brewing," he confided to John Smith when they sat in the caretaker's basement room and discussed the problem. "Somehow, I feel that this devilish business of Ackerman's will come to a head Saturday night. I could sense that in his tone when he was talking to Nancy. What he plans, I don't know—but we are the only ones who can circumvent him, John. To go to the police would mean the arrest and ruination of a lot of boys who do not realize what they are doing. We can't do that—"

"The answer is in the Nonpareil Social Club," John Smith nodded, and his angular face, even sharper than usual, was hard with anger. "I think I'd better work on it from that end."

And as Brother Henry looked at this man who in a year's time had become so invaluable to him, he thanked God for the night when it had been his privilege to use his fists to snatch John Smith out of a ganster trap that waited for him. "John Smith" had never explained that trap, if he knew why it had been set. He had never talked of his past. Instead of talking, he had taken hold of the work in the Community House and demonstrated talents and qualities which had made Brother Henry depend on him more and more completely.

"The Lindemeyer family lives just over the store where the club's located," Smith was going on with his thoughts. "They have a room to rent—back room where I can use the fire-escape. You can fix me up and I'll go around there to-morrow and rent that. Ought to be able to get a fairly good line on what Ackerman has on foot before Saturday night."

MRS. LINDEMEYER had no idea, the next morning, that the grey-haired man with the close-cropped beard, to whom she rented her spare room, was the Community House assistant with whom she had so often rubbed elbows. When Brother Henry had finished with a job of make-up, it generally was quite safe under scrutiny. Years in the theatrical profession had given him a skill at disguise he never then expected to utilize on that stern stage of life that was now his daily rostrum.

He was not apprehensive over John Smith's make-up, or about his ability to take care of himself, but, during the next two days, Brother Henry worried aplenty. Ben Reardon had disappeared from his home, seemingly vanished from the neighborhood. Had he gone into hiding because of the Caproni killing? Brother Henry feared so. Instinctively, he could feel the evil net closing around the young men of the Five Corners, the boys he had raised and trained from almost babyhood —in many cases with more pains and worry than their own parents ....

Early Saturday morning, when the Community House telephone rang and he recognized Captain Mercer's voice on the wire, an uneasy premonition told him what to expect. And he was not mistaken.

"I don't know just what to think about young Ben Reardon," the precinct captain told him, when they faced each other in the stationhouse. "That's why I asked you to come here, Brother Henry. I've been hearing things. Rumors that Ben was seen on Joe Caproni's block the night Captoni was killed. Rumors that Captoni tried to speak Reardon's name before be died.

Reardon has disappeared— you know that. I don't want to put out the dragnet for him until I'm pretty sure I'm right, but things are beginning to look bad—"

The captain's keen eyes were studying Brother Henry's face intently, alert for any sign of concealed knowledge. Brother Henry could feel the blood pounding faster in his veins, could feel it mounting in his cheeks as he mopped his bald head with a handkerchief.

"I don't know, Captain," he stammered, "but I can't believe any of my boys capable of cold-blooded murder. Give me until tonight—until midnight," he blurted suddenly. "If I can't answer your questions about Ben, then you can bring him in."

"Okay," Mercer nodded with finality, satisfied that he had enlisted the aid of a detective the equal of any on his staff. "Midnight it is—and I'm wishing you luck, Brother Henry."

He'd probably need luck and plenty of it, Brother Henry considered as he went back to the Community House. There had been nothing worth while out of John Smith so far, and his own efforts to locate Ben or to ferret out what Manny Ackerman planned had been equally unproductive ....

The telephone was clamoring as he stepped up to the door.

"I've got it, Brother Henry," John Smith's voice came excitedly. "Two or three items I've picked up listening in on the Nonpareil are beginning to click. It's a payroll robbery—and it isn't for ten-thirty tonight. It's for this morning!"

"A payroll robbery!" the words gasped unbelievingly from Brother Henry.

"The Langer Printing Company," Smith clipped the name of a large establishment located at a point where the Five Corners merged with the next community uptown. "I'm on my way over there now to see if I can spike it."

And then the receiver on the other end of the line clicked—while Brother Henry still held on to the telelphone as if he dared not put it down.

A payroll robbery—that would be no one-man job. It would require a crew—lookouts and sufficient men to cow the printing office force. That was what Manny Ackerman had been scheming; that was why he had been corrupting the youths of the Five Corners.

Brother Henry knew that he ought to call Captain Mercer and report what he had just learned—but he couldn't do that! It would mean arrest and jail for any number of overgrown youngsters who were being led into this thing without half understanding what they were doing. No, this was no job for the police!

Suddenly the receiver slammed down on its hook, and Brother Henry was racing for the door, hailing a cab, flinging himself into it. Another thought had just occurred to him; that devil Ackerman was not satisfied with corrupting the local young men—he had Nancy Carey involved in this latest outrage!

That meant that Nancy would go to jail with the rest if the police took a hand in the game ....

BROTHER HENRY'S heart sank as the taxi swept by the corner of the printing plant. Two youths he knew all too well were standing guard there—two of his boys. In front of the plant stood a big sedan with its motor running—and that was young Pete Zelinski behind the wheel. Flinging a bill at the driver, Brother Henry leaped out of the cab and raced across the sidewalk to the main doorway.

Two more young fellows were standing there—Otto Schmaller and Ernie Giesler. Hands thrust in coat pockets, they stepped forward uncertainly when they recognized him—uncertainly yet threateningly — but, before they had time to make up their minds, Brother Henry's capable hands closed around their heads, brought them crashing together with stunning force.

Then he was past them, leaping up the stone steps and flinging the big door wide. Up a long flight of steps to the office on the second floor—then at the top he met with a whirlwind of action.

To his shuddering ears came the reverberations of shots from inside the office—and then the door seemed to explode outward. For a moment, he caught a glimpse of the scene within, as if suddenly a curtain had gone up in front of him—John Smith staggering backward, collapsing to the floor in a heap. Then, Manny Ackerman materializing out of nowhere in the doorway—an automatic in his hand that came crashing down on Brother Henry's head sickeningly.

Waves of nansea swept over him as he tottered in the doorway, hands groping to grasp something, anything to save him from the sea of blackness engulfing him. He was going down . . . but somehow managed to fight his way up through the sickening vertigo.

A nightmare of horror opened his eyes. The office into which he had fallen was a shambles. Howard Langer lay slumped in death beside his desk. His secretary, also sprawling lay a few feet from the unconscious body of Ben Reardon. And Ben Reardon still clutched an automatic foul with the odor of recently burned cordite! *Ben had killed these two men!*

Sick with a despair even more overwhelming than the nauseous effect of his throbbing, giddily swimming head, Brother Henry stared around him. He realized that he had come too late. A few minutes sooner, and he might have been on time. But now ....

Unconsciously, he glanced down at his wrist-watch. It was ten-fifteen and Manny Ackerman's date with Nancy Carey was at ten-thirty! There might still be time to stop that wily devil!

BROTHER HENRY'S throbbing head threatened to burst as he thudded jarringly down that flight of steps to the street. No cab was in sight, so frantically, he started to run, though it seemed that the swaying, pitching sidewalk must rise up and send him headlong at any moment. It was blocks and blocks to that stable-garage that housed Manny Ackerman's car. Yet, as he thought about it. he was convinced that his hunch was certain. Ackerman was a yellow crook, a contemptible double-crosser who would cheerfully betray the young fools he had lured into crime ....

Block after panting block—then that stable was just ahead. The door stood open. Was he too late? Had Ackerman already been there and made his escape, or would the canary-colored car come roaring out at any moment?

Vile oaths had never sounded so sweet to Brother Henry as when he lurched up to that doorway—vicious curses in Manny Ackerman's snarling voice.

Brother Henry glimpsed the man, himself, as he suddenly appeared in the doorway, mean eyes slitted with rage. Nancy was beside him, clinging to his arm.

"You can't go! You can't leave me now, Manny!" she pleaded. "We can get a taxi—we can take a train! There must be some way—"

Ackerman whirled on her viciously. "Damn you!" he spat at her. "I told you I haven't got any time to fool with you! Get out of my way or—"

Suddenly, his hand lashed out, slapped her across the face so savagely that she staggered back against the stable wall. A trickle of blood ran from her mouth.

The sound of that slap was as a bomb bursting in Brother Henry's brain; Nancy's blood like a red haze before his eyes. Exhaustion dropped from him, the pain and dizziness of his swollen head forgotten. He threw himself at Ackerman, diving low to avoid the automatic coming up from the fellow's hip pocket.

Viciously, the weapon swiped at the bald pate it had almost cracked a short while before, but this time Brother Henry's fingers closed around the gun-wrist and stopped it in mid-air—stopped it and forced it back inexorably, with strength that would not be denied. Ackerman cursed frenziedly. His knee jack-knifed treacherously as he tried to rake Brother Henry's face with his free hand—and then he was screaming like a woman as the tortured arm went back, back, until the bone snapped.

Biting, spitting, snarling like a wounded beast, the pain-tortured crook rolled on the floor, using every trick of the underworld brawler's repertoire as he struggled to break away. But now Brother Henry was sure of his man. From the corners of his eyes, he had glimpsed the gay-colored car. He had seen that all four of its tires were flat. Those tires were gashed and torn so that they could not possibly be used again. Then, with methodical deliberation, he pounded Manny Ackerman into insensibility.

Nancy Carey was still cowering, weeping, against the wall, handkerchief held to her bleeding mouth as she half-crouched over the suitcase which contained her clothing. But now there was a new light in her tear-reddened eyes—a light of full awakening, belated understanding. It told Brother Henry that now she saw Manny Ackerman as he actually was.

"Pull yourself together, Nancy," he said quietly. "Go see if you can locate a taxi. I don't trust a snake like this even when he's unconscious."

THE police were in charge when the taxicab rolled to a stop in front of the Langer Printing Company's plant, and they welcomed Manny Ackerman with open arms. Quickly, Brother Henry cast a worried eye over the set-up in the robbed office—and what he saw there filled him with profound relief.

John Smith was alive. An ambulance surgeon had dressed a bullet wound in his shoulder, but except for that he seemed none the worse for his battle. Ben Reardon, too, was sitting up in one of the office chairs with a bandage around his forehead—but he was smiling up at Nancy. Also, except for Ben there were none of the duped youths in evidence.

"There he is, Sergeant," Smith nodded to O'Malley when Manny Ackerman was dragged in. "He's the answer to half a dozen crimes during the past month—just smart aleck hold-ups to show the kids how easy it was. The slick crook planned this job today and figured to slip off with the proceeds while he left Ben Reardon holding the bag for him."

"And I believed him!" Nancy broke into hysterical sobs as, somehow, she found her way over to Ben Reardon's chair. "I didn't know anything about this, Ben. I didn't know that he was tricking you into a robbery and then planning to run out on you—"

"But he wasn't tricking me into anything," Reardon grinned as his arm went around her. "I didn't like Ackerman the moment I saw him, honey. When I saw that he was playing up to you, I knew I'd have to do something about it. I suspected all along that he was pulling these robberies in the Five Corners—especially, when he handed out money so liberally to the boys in the Nonpareil Club. But I couldn't get anything definite on him. I almost caught him when he killed Joe Caproni, but I got there just too late to save Joe's life.

"He managed to tell me who he thought the hold-up man was—and I made up my mind that the next time I'd trap him so red-handed there'd be no slip-up. That's why I came up here today, when I got wind of this stick-up. But Ackerman was too slick for me. He thought he had left me lying there framed as the murderer of Langer and his secretary; but I was one jump ahead of him. I had already taken care of the tires of his car, just in case he managed to slip through my fingers again—"

Suddenly, Reardon's expression changed, became apologetic, and his eyes turned appreciatively to where Brother Henry was talking with Mercer.

"Looks as if I wasn't so darned clever at that," he admitted ruefully. "Ackerman would have gotten clear away at the last minute if Brother Henry hadn't been on hand to nab him."

But Brother Henry hardly heard him, for the police captain was just summing up the case to his entire satisfaction.

"Seems as if this Nonpareil Club bunch were being played for a lot of suckers," Captain Mercer nodded wisely. "I haven't any evidence that they were actually in on any of these crimes, you understand. But maybe you'd better take them in hand and teach them the error of their ways, Brother Henry. Looks to me as if you're a pretty good teacher—of quite a number of things."

And the broad wink with which he finished, as he glanced from Brother Henry's swollen fists to the chair that was doing double duty for Ben Reardon and Nancy Carey, might have been interpreted in a number of ways.

THE END

DEADLY FOES OF THE SPIDER

HE was known only as THE DEVIL Hand, because he inflicted hideous death merely by LOOKING at his victims, no one ever lived to describe him! So great was his incredible cunning that he hid behind the authority of the Mayor; behind the honor of the Police Department -- even behind the sinister cloak of the SPIDER!

Originally appeared in
MURDER'S LEGIONNAIRES
THE SPIDER, Feb. 1942

THE MASTER OF MEN! SPIDER

Here's a checklist of the original SPIDER pulp magazines! All collector's items, and destined to appear in new editions from BOLD VENTURE PRESS!

NEXT:

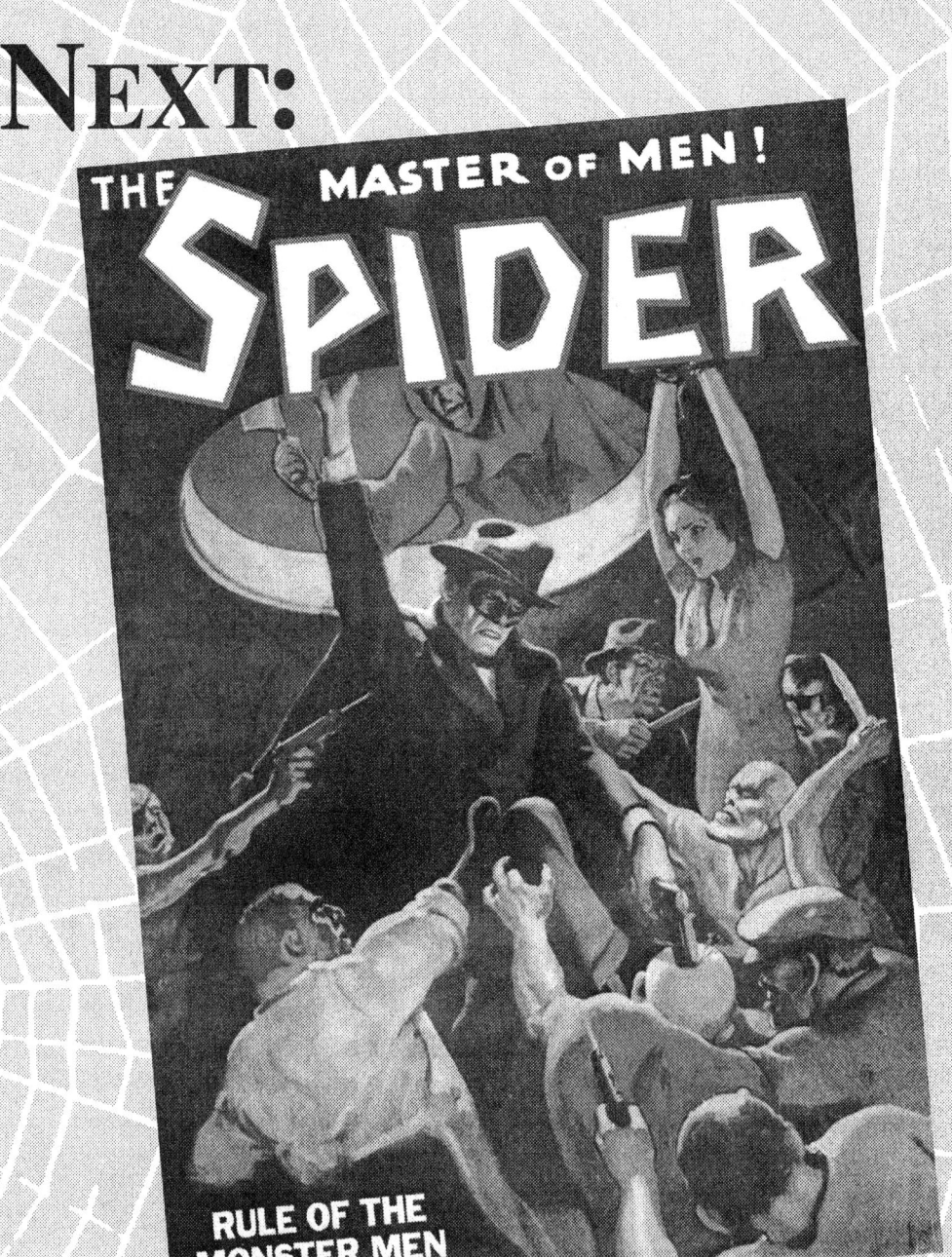

"Rule of the Monster Men"

Transformed by an Underworld sadist — The Wreck — into a city of man-made, outlaw cripples, New York faces the gravest criminal threat of all time. No area is safe — not even the World's Fair! Can the *Spider*, already robbed of his most loyal assistant, save a great metropolis from madness and death?

On sale February 15th, 2002